THE DRAGON'S TRIANGLE

THE DRAGON'S TRIANGLE

The True Story of the First Nonstop Flight
Across the Pacific

DAVID ROSTEN

The Dragon's Triangle
The True Story of the First Nonstop Flight Across the Pacific

Library of Congress Control Number: 2015919573
ISBN: Hardcover   978-1-5144-2989-1
               Softcover   978-1-5144-2988-4
               eBook   978-1-5144-2986-0

Print information available on the last page.

Rev. date: 12/01/2015

To order additional copies of this book, contact:
Xlibris
1-888-795-4274
www.Xlibris.com
Orders@Xlibris.com
723044

Dedication

I dedicate this book to my children and to the memory of my mother and father, Philip and Leila Rosten. There are a few other remarkable people who have purposefully helped to bring us into a safer and more secure world. I embrace their spirit of adventure and their quest for knowledge. To Ray Chambers, United Nations Secretary-General's Special Envoy for Malaria. He personally has saved over one million lives attributed to his efforts for the eradication of malaria in Africa. To Daniel Wehrenfennig, director of the Olive Tree Initiative. To Paula Garb and David Snow, co-directors of the Center for Citizenpeacebuilding, who envision a more peaceful world through understanding.

Author's Note

This story is based on true events. There are creative liberties taken with some of the characters. However, the events are true, and the information regarding the historic flight is accurate.

Preface

Years ago, I read about the first transpacific flight. I had never heard of Clyde Pangborn and Hugh Herndon Jr.'s flight across the Pacific. Most people had heard of Charles Lindbergh's flight across the Atlantic and Amelia Earhart's subsequent transatlantic flight. The more I researched, I realized that the Pangborn/Herndon flight was more interesting than the Lindbergh flight in many ways because it was longer and more difficult technically.

In 1931, most people in the United States were focused on where they were going to get their next meal. At the time about 25 percent of the working population of America was unemployed.

Later on, in 1932, the twenty-month-old son of Charles and Anne Lindbergh was kidnapped on the first of March from their home in New Jersey, and the country became focused on the "Lindbergh kidnapping." On April second, Charles Lindbergh turned over $50,000 as a ransom for the safe return of his kidnapped son, and on May twelfth, the boy was found dead on the side of a New Jersey road by a truck driver. The country was left reeling from this murder.

The country needed a hero in the midst of the Lindbergh kidnapping and the depth of the Great Depression. On May 20, 1932, eight days after Charles Lindbergh Jr. was found dead, Amelia Earhart left Newfoundland and became the first woman to fly solo across the Atlantic. The country had found their hero.

The news of the Pangborn/Herndon flight of October 1931 was lost to history. Part of the reason the flight was overlooked is that the chief pilot Clyde Pangborn was under a gag order, which did not allow him to speak about the flight until October 1932.

This is the story of the first transpacific flight.

Chapter 1

Princeton University, 1930

The campus is covered in a blanket of autumn leaves. The brisk air has the smell of impending winter as a cool breeze blows across campus.

Alice Boardman is all business. She's a forty-year-old socialite and heiress to the Standard Oil and Tidewater fortune. Her twenty-year-old son Hugh is a student at the university, and she arrives for a visit in her new 1930 16-cylinder Cadillac. Going straight to the Blair Hall college dorm, she walks upstairs and knocks on her son's door.

Hugh's girlfriend, Mary Ellen, answers the door. Scantily clad, she very much looks the part of typical sorority girl after a long evening.

Mary Ellen asks, "Who are you?"

Alice, dressed as usual for business, will allow nothing, including a twenty-year-old sorority girl, to ruffle her feathers this morning.

"Wake my son up," Alice answers.

Mary Ellen looks at Hugh's mother all dressed up in her fine mink stole. This is a test of will, and it appears Mary Ellen wants to have the last word. With a condescending tone that takes years of practice for proper delivery and intonation during moments like this, Mary Ellen replies, "You must be his mother."

Alice, who has no patience for this will of wits so early in the morning, walks straight past Mary Ellen.

Mary Ellen scoffs and says, "Well, come on in."

Hugh is lying halfway off the bed in a silk robe. Empty bottles of fine whiskey are strewn about his dorm room, which is an actual crime because of the Prohibition laws in place. Several ashtrays with cigarette and cigar butts litter the room, and clothes have been tossed everywhere.

The country is in the middle of the Depression, and it is apparent that Hugh and his mother are completely insensitive to the plight of the country.

"This is a disgrace. Wake up!" Alice says.

Hugh opens up an eye when his mother shakes him awake.

Hugh asks, "What are you doing here, Mother?"

Alice, annoyed, reminds him that she told him she was going to visit this week.

With sleep still heavy in his voice, he says, "I'm leaving Princeton, Mother."

Taken aback, Alice says, "What do you mean you are leaving Princeton?"

"I'm going to fly airplanes," he says with a sheepish grin.

Alice is appalled. "You cannot just drop out of school to fly airplanes!"

Hugh picks up a cigarette, lights it, and blows several smoke rings. "I really don't like academics."

"You know our family has a legacy here at Princeton. I forbid you to leave."

"I don't need your permission, Mother. I am a grown man now and I am not an academic."

"I forbid you to disgrace yourself and the family in this way. I am taking away your airplane."

"Oh, I am really scared now, Mother."

Mary Ellen laughs, and Alice glares at her, then asks, "What are you laughing at?" Mary Ellen doesn't say a word. Hugh's mother continues her attack and tells Mary Ellen, "Would you be so kind to gather your clothes and what a little bit of dignity you have left, and leave?"

Mary Ellen is steadfast and not swayed by Alice's rancor or her judgment. "I am in love with your son, and we are getting married. So I'll just take my clothes, thank you."

By the time Mary Ellen leaves, every strand of hair is perfectly positioned and there is not a wrinkle on her clothes.

"Hugh, I purchased a new Standard D-24 and you crashed it. Where's the new plane?"

"I was going to speak with you about that, Mother," Hugh says, wincing as he relates the details of crashing his new plane.

Chapter 2

Gates Flying Circus
Ft. Monmouth, NJ

Several weeks later, the Gates Flying Circus has come to town. During this time of the Depression, the circus is a huge event with people arriving from hundreds of miles around. The people are happy to have a diversion from the economic crisis the country is in.

Being interested in everything having to do with flight, Hugh plans to go and asks his mother if she would like to go with him. She agrees, and later in the day, they arrive at the Gates Flying Circus. They are amazed by the number of people in attendance as they make their way to the grandstands. Hundreds of spectators are in the stands watching the planes flying over the field, and still more are walking around with their children, playing arcade games. A Gates Flying Circus banner is stretched across the road, and excitement fills the air.

Bill Brooks, a thirty-something pilot for the circus, calls out to the crowd, "Step right up, ladies and gentlemen. Don't be afraid. This isn't our first time flying and I hope it's not our last."

Most people in the country are struggling just to feed their family, and the airshow is a way to take their minds off of their hunger and the lack of opportunity. Families scrape together any money they can to see the airshow.

"Purchase a ticket for the world-famous One Dollar Joy Ride. This is the opportunity of a lifetime. There are a limited number of tickets available, so don't waste any time," Bill continues.

Air travel is in its infancy at this time, so some people had never even seen an airplane fly, but for one dollar, they could actually fly in one. It really was the opportunity of a lifetime for most, so many patrons came to the circus for the sole purpose of taking advantage of this special, and the line of people waiting to purchase tickets was long.

The owner of the circus, Ivan Gates, who is a little overweight from spending too many of his forty years drinking heavily, is at the podium in front of the grandstands. He's dressed in a coat and tie, with a hat atop his head, and has a mustache on his face.

With a megaphone Ivan speaks to the crowd, "Ladies and gentlemen, today you will see death-defying stunts never performed before."

Hugh and the other onlookers are excited to see the first stunt in the show is an automobile-to-airplane transfer. A cruising airplane with a rope ladder flies over the field, and the well-known pilot Clyde Pangborn grabs the ladder and climbs into the aircraft. The crowd is wild with delight, clapping and cheering.

Twenty-four-year-old Diane steps into the line to purchase a ticket. Her long blonde hair is tied back in a ponytail, and her beautiful slender figure, in a yellow sundress, does not go unnoticed by passersby.

When Diane reaches the front of the line, she asks Bill, "Are you sure it's safe?"

"My dear, I have flown nine hundred and eighty people in one day, and the Gates Flying Circus has flown hundreds of thousands of people with a perfect safety record. And I'm not exaggerating. Ivan Gates is a stickler for details; he hires only the best and safest pilots," he says with a smile.

Diane is convinced and says, "Well, in that case, I would like to purchase a ticket."

Bill smiles again and looks down at the ticket before handing it to her. "Young lady, you just won yourself a free ticket! Enjoy the ride."

"Really? Are you sure?" she says, elated.

Handing her the ticket, he says, "Yes ma'am, you're really the winner."

Diane takes the free ticket, squirming with delight. "Thank you!"

At thirty years old, Clyde Pangborn is already a well-known aviator. He is handsome, tall, and lanky. The plane he flies is the Standard J-1, which has an enlarged front cockpit to hold four passengers. *Flying Gates Circus* is painted on the side of the plane with *Upside-Down Pangborn* painted on a second line.

A steel ladder is permanently bolted on both sides of the passenger cockpit, so new passengers can load on one side while other passengers disembark on the other side.

Diane is in line waiting to board the Standard J-1, and Bill helps her onto the airplane once Clyde lands to pick up new passengers. Clyde takes off in the Standard and flies a large circle around the airstrip and then lands.

As Diane is getting off the plane, she blushes as she tells Clyde, "Thank you." Clyde is a little taken with her and tells her that she's welcome.

Ivan Gates gets the crowd excited for the next act.

"Ladies and gentlemen, the world-famous, the one and only Clyde Pangborn will perform the death-defying change of plane while in flight."

Just then two biplanes travel toward each other from opposite sides of the field. It looks like they are going to collide. At the last moment, one of the planes turns upside down and the two planes narrowly miss the other.

Flying five feet over the landing strip in front of the spectators, Pangborn goes barreling down the airfield, then flies straight up into the air.

The crowd gasps as they watch this daring aerial stunt.

Ivan continues, "Here they come for the one and only plane-to-plane transfer."

The crowd is on the edge of their seats as two planes fly over the field, and Clyde climbs out of the top plane to stand on the lower wing. From the lower wing, he lets himself down on top of the top wing of the lower airplane.

He then lets himself down into the open-air cockpit as the two planes veer off in opposite directions at the end of the field.

The crowd goes wild as they see this maneuver.

Hugh says, "Mother, I really want to fly for the Gates Flying Circus."

Alice stares at him, her mouth hanging open, unable to believe his words. "You most certainly are not flying for any circus. I did not raise you to be a common circus performer! It's bad enough that you have dropped out of school. You could at least find some reputable way to pursue a career in flying."

"I will just have to join the military to gain experience. I am old enough now. I want to fly."

Alice relents. She thinks that it's better to have him home than possibly being sent away to war in the military.

"Let's speak with the owner of the show. This looks better than having people shooting at you."

Hugh walks up to Bill and asks, "Who's the owner of the circus?"

"Is something wrong, my good man?" Bill asks.

"I just want to speak with the owner about flying planes."

"Lots of pilots are looking for work. Don't get your hopes up," he responds and points to Ivan Gates. "Good luck."

Hugh and Alice go up to Ivan Gates. Alice takes charge and introduces herself and her son. "This is my son Hugh and he'd like to fly for you."

Ivan is certainly used to having people who want to fly approach him. During this time in history, everyone wants to fly. Everyone wants to get into an airplane. "Son, you don't look like a pilot to me."

Alice tells Mr. Gates that her son isn't much of a pilot. "He has already wrecked two planes."

Ivan decides to scare her. "Why didn't you say this before? Maybe he would be good. The crowd wants to see blood."

Alice is jolted by his words and says, "Perhaps you could suggest another career for my son." Ivan jokingly tells Hugh and his mother to look up. "Maybe Hugh can be a parachutist."

Rosalie Gordon is a nineteen-year-old friend of Michael Hunt, Clyde's copilot. She has been telling Michael that she wants to be a parachutist and jump off a plane.

The three of them are in Clyde's plane, with Clyde at the controls. The plane takes off down the runway and lumbers into the air as music from the band on the ground plays. Rosalie is in the front seat and waves to the audience as they do a flyover. The crowd waves back in anticipation of what's to come.

Clyde takes the plane up to two thousand feet. He looks at Rosalie and yells over the engine noise of the plane, "Remember to jump out away from the wing."

Rosalie looks nervous and she nods her head.

She climbs up onto the wing. Clyde is getting nervous too, sensing that it is unwise to take an inexperienced young lady up to perform a wing walk. What if she freezes or falls? Clyde didn't want to think about that. Michael insists she will be ok, and Rosalie is enthusiastic about doing the stunt. Clyde gives in and lets her attempt the stunt.

When Rosalie jumps, the shrouds of her parachute get stuck in the wings.

From down below, the crowd sees Rosalie hanging from behind the plane.

Michael tries to pull her back into the plane. He shouts, "I can't pull her in, Clyde."

Clyde shouts over the wind and engine noise, "Let's switch places. You fly the plane straight and I'll try to pull her in." Michael and Clyde struggle to change positions. Clyde gets up on the wing as Michael struggles to keep the plane flying level.

The weight of Rosalie combined with the forces of dragging through the air make it impossible to pull her in.

"Are you all right?" Clyde yells to Rosalie. She is frozen with fear and does not answer. "Rosalie, we are going to get you," says Clyde.

Clyde gets back into the cockpit and takes the controls of the plane. He performs a pass over the runway.

The crowd thinks that it is part of the show, and they cheer. Ivan Gates, knowing this isn't part of the act, directs Freddy Lund, one of the other circus pilots, to get in another airplane.

"Jump into your plane and get up there, Freddy!"

Freddy says, "Yes, boss," and starts up his plane.

With a puff of smoke, the plane goes down the grass field and lifts off. Freddy quickly pulls up next to Clyde's plane. Freddy and his copilot Milton Girton do a plane-to-plane transfer with Clyde.

They position their plane next to Clyde's wing, and Milton transfers to Clyde's plane. Clyde and Milton are able to pull Rosalie in safely. Both planes land safely, and Clyde says to Rosalie, "You're all right now."

"I don't know what to say. You saved my life!" Rosalie says to them. The crowd goes wild as the four of them get off the plane. Photographers come running up to them to take their picture. Clyde is calm, going about his normal postflight business, checking the plane and the fuel.

Later, a reporter asks Clyde, "Do you have anything to say after saving that girl's life?"

Clyde tells him, "We were all lucky. There was no gas left in the tank."

Diane is standing among the crowd and makes her way up to Clyde. "That was really remarkable today."

"It really was," Clyde answers.

He looks up and sees that Diane is beautiful. Not only beautiful but he thinks she seems really sweet as well.

Playing a little hard to get, he asks Diane if he flew her earlier in the day, but Diane knows that he noticed her. "I know that you saw me on your plane earlier today. I'm the one who won the free flight."

Clyde says, "I'm sorry. I did notice you and didn't forget you. Since you won the free flight, come back tomorrow and I could take you for a longer ride."

"I don't know if I can. I'm a nurse, and I'm scheduled to work at the hospital."

Clyde nervously asks her, "What time do you get off work?"

"I should be off around 3:00."

"Come by after you finish. I'll take you then."

Diane is excited and says, "That would be incredible. See you tomorrow."

"What's your name?" asks Clyde.

Diane tells Clyde her name, and he says, "My name is Clyde."

Diane laughs and says, "I know. It's written on the side of the plane."

After the photographers leave, Hugh approaches Clyde and introduces himself. Clyde looks at Hugh all dressed up like a preppy and says, "What can I do for you?"

"I have been reading about you. That was quite an amazing rescue."

Clyde says, "Thanks."

"I mean it. It was unbelievable. I would really like to join the flying circus."

"You need to speak with Gates. I'm just a pilot," Clyde answers. Just like Ivan, he is used to hearing requests from wannabe pilots.

"I already spoke with Mr. Gates. He says he isn't looking for any pilots. I thought you might know of a way to help me out."

Clyde sees that Alice and Hugh are very well dressed. "Don't you know lots of experienced pilots are out of work? This country is in an economic depression, and there are no jobs for anyone. The country is suffering, and many people wait in long lines just to get food. Nearly thirty million have lost their jobs. Twenty-five percent of the population of Washington State is out of work. And you want to just show up and say you want a job?" Clyde responded, incredulous.

Hugh hands Clyde his business card. "Contact me if something comes up."

Clyde rolls his eyes. He's not the first person to be annoyed by Hugh's cavalier attitude and pretty attire.

The next day, late in the afternoon, Diane comes back to the circus to see Clyde. When she finds him, she taps him on the shoulder and sweetly says, "Hi."

Clyde turns around and is pleasantly surprised to see her. He says, "I was hoping you were going to come back." He grins ear to ear.

"I'm sorry I'm late. I got busy at the hospital. I hope it's not too late for the airplane ride."

"It is actually perfect timing. The crowd has left the airfield, and I'm just checking the plane. Let me help you into the plane."

Diane is surprised. "Really?"

"Really," he says and chuckles at her excitement.

Diane takes note of the people surrounding Clyde and the attention he's getting. "Do you take young single women on rides in the airplane often?"

"Well, that's what I do for a living!" They both laugh.

Clyde helps her into the plane. Milton comes out from a hangar and helps him start the engine as Clyde jumps into the plane.

Milton says, "Contact."

The engine comes to life and Clyde taxis down the runway. There is a loud backfire; a puff of smoke comes out of the exhaust. Milton jumps out of the way and Clyde gives some throttle. The plane gains speed and immediately lifts off.

The afternoon sky turns vivid colors of red and orange as the plane takes to the air.

As the plane gains altitude, Diane throws her arms up in the air, exhilarated.

"I am flying!" she yells.

Clyde takes the plane for a steep turn and goes out toward the ocean.

Over the engine noise, she says, "I can't believe I can see the ocean. It's so beautiful from up here!"

"Are you all right? There is a blanket under the seat if you are cold," Clyde says.

"I'm fine. This is amazing!"

Clyde turns the plane back toward the airfield and lands. As the plane is taxiing, Diane says, "Thank you for flying me in your plane again."

"You're welcome. I wonder if you would like to have dinner with me tonight?"

Diane smiles. "I would love that," she answers as Clyde helps her out of the plane.

Chapter 3

Long Branch, NJ

As Clyde and Diane sit down at a table with red, checkered tablecloths in a small Italian restaurant, she says, "That was so much fun today. It really was one of the greatest moments of my life."

"I really enjoyed it too. Thank you for coming back. You know what I do. Why don't you tell me a little bit about your work?" Clyde says.

"I love helping people. That's why I became a nurse."

"Where do you work?"

"I work at a local hospital. My family lives here too. Where does your family live?"

"My mother lives in Washington State."

"Is it hard to be on the road?"

"It is hard. I love the flying, but it would be great to settle down someday."

"Why haven't you?"

"I haven't met the right person." He grins and says, "Why haven't you found someone yet?"

Diane nods. "It's the same for me. I have been focused on family and work. I don't know where the time goes."

"I totally understand. It's been difficult for me to balance family and work too."

"I have really enjoyed having dinner with you, but I must head home now," Diane says, reluctant to part ways.

Clyde, sad to see the evening end, says, "Thank you. Let's stay in touch. We're leaving tomorrow."

"I would enjoy that too."

Chapter 4

Alice Herndon Estate

Hugh drives through the gates of his family home and up the treelined driveway. The last of the autumn leaves have fallen from the trees.

Hugh gets out of his car and walks up to the front door. Alice opens the door and says, "We were expecting you."

Hugh looks sincerely happy to be home. "Nice to see you, Mother."

"We are hosting several other families for Thanksgiving dinner. Some of them have proper daughters that I plan to introduce you to."

Hugh tells his mother emphatically, "Please don't, Mother. I am engaged to Mary Ellen."

"Before you marry anyone, you are required to return to school and complete your studies."

Hugh pulls the daily newspaper out of his jacket pocket. On the front page of the newspaper is the headline "Upside-Down Pangborn Saves Girl in the Sky." Clyde is a national hero. "Mother, did you see the headlines?"

Alice looks at the newspaper. "I read the newspaper like everyone else. Why do they excite and sensationalize the sentiments of people by publishing this garbage?"

Hugh is not surprised by his mother's response. Alice generally doesn't have many nice things to say about other people, and any other response by his mother would have been completely out of character. "Mother, he is on the front page of all the national papers."

Alice replies, "Upside-Down Pangborn, or whatever they call him, is just a flash in the pan. You'll never see his name in the news again."

Chapter 5

The Business of Flying

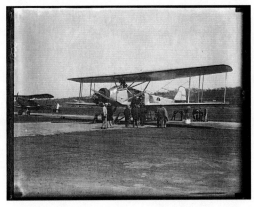

Several days later, Hugh tells his mother he sent "Upside-Down Pangborn" a note after meeting him at the circus. "He replied that he might be interested in starting another airshow. Isn't that exciting, Mother?"

"I have been doing some checking on my own and found out the owner of the flying circus, in spite of his success, is having financial difficulties. Our sources say Ivan Gates is not interested in selling the circus. Did the upside-down guy specify his terms?"

Hugh tells his mother, "Partners, of course. We provide the money. He provides the experience." His excitement is nearly tangible.

Alice asks curtly, "How do we get our investment returned?"

"I will have our attorneys draw up a contract. He will have no choice but to sign if he wants to do this. We purchase the planes. If the upside-down guy doesn't pay us, we take the planes," he says.

"Finally, you're speaking my language, Hugh."

Several days later, Clyde is working on some of the planes with the mechanics, getting them ready for the next airshow, and Hugh shows up at the airfield. Clyde sees Hugh and walks over to him. "Looks like you are here to do some business."

"I spoke with my family," says Hugh. "They gave me the go-ahead to purchase a few planes."

Clyde holds his hand out to shake Hugh's. "That's fantastic news. What should we call the business?"

"I wrote down several names. I like the name 'The Flying Fleet,' " Hugh says, beaming.

"Before we really begin this endeavor, I need to speak with Mr. Gates first, out of consideration for our long relationship. My friend, I have a feeling we might be able to accomplish more than just starting a circus."

Chapter 6

The Fight

Ivan is sitting in his office doing paperwork at his desk when Clyde comes in. Ivan's wife, Sandy, is lounging in a chair in the corner.

"I've got some bad news. I was thinking, Ivan, and I believe that it's time for me to leave the circus."

Ivan looks up from his desk, and his face turns a shade of red. "We are doing great together. Why would you want out?"

"I just want out. Nothing personal."

"Why would you want out?" he asks again. "We have a dozen airplanes and twenty performers."

"We have done great together, Ivan. I am just tired."

Ivan is a little taken aback and says, "Tired? Tired of what?"

"I told you, I don't want to make it personal."

"I want to know," Ivan says, intent on getting an answer.

Clyde huffs. "I'll just say it. I am tired of your drinking, and I'm tired of your gambling."

"That is none of your business," Ivan retorts, feeling defensive.

"Ok, then. Where is the five hundred dollars you were saving for me from last week? Is it still under your mattress?"

Ivan is silent as Clyde continues, "You see, it is my business. You gambled it away. That was *my* money."

"We'll get it back," Ivan answers sheepishly.

Clyde is right, but he doesn't know when to stop. "All gamblers think they will get it back, and they end up broke. We won't get the money back. I want out, Ivan."

Ivan pulls out a gun and points it at Clyde.

"What are you doing? Are you going to shoot me?"

Sandy has been watching this entire exchange. "Ivan. Put away the gun," she says.

Ivan tells her, "This is my game. You don't tell me how to play my game."

Clyde puts his hands up in mock surrender. "Put away the gun before someone gets hurt," he says.

Ivan keeps the revolver aimed at Clyde. "You get out of here, Clyde, before *you* get hurt."

Clyde rushes Ivan. Ivan takes a shot but misses. He takes several more shots, but Clyde is on top of him, attempting to get the gun away.

Ivan swings the butt of the pistol and smashes the side of Clyde's face. Clyde is immediately knocked out cold.

A week later, Clyde wakes up in the hospital. His jaw is wired shut. He looks around and sees Sandy in the room with him. Clyde tries to speak but can't.

"Don't move. You had a severe concussion." She stops for a moment and continues, "Ivan says he's sorry."

Clyde mumbles something, trying to ask Sandy how long he has been in the hospital.

"You have been in the hospital for a week, and your jaw is going to be wired shut for three months."

Sandy gives Clyde a writing pad and pen.

Clyde begins to put it all together. He is obviously upset, scribbling furiously on the note pad. He hands the paper to Sandy.

Ivan tried to kill me. I am out.

Sandy replies, "He just loses his temper. He can't help it. He doesn't trust me or anyone else."

They hear a knock at the door, and Diane comes into the hospital room, wearing her nursing uniform. "I guess you can't get away from me now."

Clyde tries to smile but can't.

Later, Ivan and Sandy are at their modest apartment. Model airplanes are all around the apartment on shelves, tables, and the counter. Promotional posters of the Gates Flying Circus are strewn about.

Ivan looks at Sandy. With a sigh, he says, "I am tired of running the flying circus."

Sandy says, "Why don't you just sell the business to Clyde? We can be happy together."

"How is Clyde, by the way?"

"He finally woke up. He still wants to quit the circus."

"Is he very upset with me?" Ivan asks, hanging his head.

"He probably is, and for good reason. Clyde will probably forgive you when he is a little better."

"Do you think he's going to file criminal charges?"

"I don't think so. That's not who Clyde is."

"When you see Clyde again, tell him once again that I'm sorry. I'm going to get some fresh air."

Ivan walks over to the balcony of their apartment, stretches out his arms, and takes in a deep breath of fresh air. Then he jumps from their seventh-floor balcony.

Chapter 7

The Airplane

Several Months Later
The Bellanca Aircraft Corporation Factory
Wilmington, Delaware

Giuseppe Bellanca, the first person to build an airplane in Italy, had moved to the United States and eventually started his own business building airplanes.

Giuseppe comes out from his office to the waiting room where Clyde and Hugh are waiting to meet with him.

"Good morning, gentlemen. It is very nice to meet you. Thank you for visiting the factory," Giuseppe says, extending his hand.

Clyde takes his hand. "Good morning, Mr. Bellanca. It is a pleasure to meet you. I'm Clyde Pangborn and this is my partner, Hugh Herndon."

Hugh shakes Mr. Bellanca's hand.

"Mr. Pangborn and Mr. Herndon. Please call me Giuseppe. I would like to give you a tour of the factory."

"That would really be incredible. Thank you," Clyde says.

"First, I would like to say that I'm sorry about your partner Mr. Gates," says Giuseppe.

"Thank you. I am sorry too. He was a good friend, and he suffered from depression for a long time."

"I followed the safety record of the Gates Flying Circus, and I was always amazed with the number of flights that you all did without any serious accidents."

"Mr. Gates' first priority was safety. The planes were inspected each day. He checked the quality of the fuel, the filters, and the flying conditions. He believed if there was ever an accident, it would be pilot error and would not be attributed to mechanical failure. He believed in the quality of the planes, and he hired only the best pilots available."

"The Bellanca company specializes in building fast and efficient light aircraft; however, anyone can build a fast aircraft, but what about the quality of the plane? I take a personal interest in every plane we design from the quality of the metal, to the fasteners and rivets. We purchase and inspect every inch of the aircraft to be certain that any aircraft that bears my name is the highest quality in design and materials available. The Bellanca CF is such an aircraft. Based on the success of the CF, I was hired to design an aircraft to fit the J-5 Whirlwind engine. It is really the most reliable aircraft engine available today."

Clyde thinks for a moment. "I never understood this. The plane was designed around the engine?"

Giuseppe chuckles. "It really was. Italians take great pride in the things we make. If it is a product that you are proud of, you put your name on it. Italians don't hide behind company names. My company is a personal reflection of me." Giuseppe stops in front of one of the planes being developed. "Charles Lindbergh tried to purchase a Bellanca CF exactly like this one for his transatlantic trip. He understood design and realized that the weight-to-power ratio was perfect for his epic flight.

"Lindbergh and I did not get along well and could not agree on terms, so Lindbergh walked away and took his business to Ryan Aircraft. Of course the rest is history with the *Spirit of St. Louis* also powered by a Wright Whirlwind engine.

"A Wright-Bellanca plane named the *Miss Columbia* did make a transatlantic flight from New York to Berlin two weeks later. By then, you know, Lindbergh was known the world over."

"That's why we are here. I studied both planes, and I believe the *Miss Columbia* flight was more interesting technically because it was made with a general purpose airplane that seats more than one passenger. I saw the only modification for the transatlantic flight was the rear seats being taken out and replaced with extra fuel tanks."

"You know your planes," says Giuseppe. "In comparison, the *Spirit of St. Louis* was built specifically for the transatlantic flight and carried only one passenger in an awkward blind cockpit. I was able to find some financial backers and build airplanes that I designed. The planes that you see here in the factory are the descendants of the *Miss Columbia*," says Giuseppe.

"I am impressed by the workmanship, and I'd like to purchase one of your planes," Clyde says.

"You have done your homework? What are you going to use it for?"

"Before we begin building our flying circus, we are going to attempt to break the round-the-world speed record. We will need it customized, but we think your design is the best," Clyde answers.

"I do too. What type of customizing are your thinking of?"

Clyde says, "Your standard plane has two 108-gallon tanks. We need auxiliary tanks to increase the range."

"That is exactly what it requires. We'll need to cut down the weight in other areas if you increase the fuel load."

"Take the weight off anywhere you like," Clyde says.

"Then we will design a flying fuel tank. It will be a flying engine with controls. It won't be our luxury model." Giuseppe laughs.

"Nice. That is just what we need," Clyde says, laughing.

"The plane will be powered by a Wright J-6 super engine. I believe the cruise speed will be ninety-five miles per hour. The plane will be rated for one hundred sixty miles per hour."

Clyde is impressed. "If the plane is overloaded with an additional six hundred pounds of fuel, will the airframe hold?"

"We will make sure the wings don't fall off. As you know, the plane is built from spruce, and we will use the best grade of spruce available."

"According to my calculations, we need to be sure it can carry at least seven hundred gallons of fuel, plus fifteen gallons of lubricating oil," Clyde says.

"This is going to be expensive, my friend."

Hugh says, "We have support from my family. We also have sponsorship from Associated Oil Company and Veedol Motor Oil."

"Looks like we are in business, gentlemen," Giuseppe says.

"We want the name *Miss Veedol* painted on the plane. We also have a sponsorship from Texaco, so we need their logo on the plane too," Hugh says.

Giuseppe shakes each man's hand again and says, "A pleasure to do business with you both. Your plane will be ready in six weeks."

Chapter 8

Six Weeks Later
Bellanca Factory

Hugh and Clyde are in the waiting room of the Bellanca factory once again, and Giuseppe comes out of his office. The new plane is parked in the showroom.

"Great to see you both," Giuseppe says as he approaches the men and motions for them to follow him to the showroom.

Hugh and Clyde follow him to the showroom and look over the plane.

"Pretty amazing?" Giuseppe asks.

"I'm stunned," Clyde answers. Hugh is obviously excited by how the plane turned out. Giuseppe smiles, glad they are pleased with the work.

"One of the unique features is the four wing struts that were molded into the small wings by adding an airfoil shape to them," Giuseppe explains. "They are aligned with the airflow during cruise so they create less drag. At low speeds and during takeoff and landing, the struts are at an angle of attack to add more lifting surface to the airplane and allow a slower takeoff speed."

"It's sheer genius," Clyde says.

"We also devised a way to counter the high lift created. The large nose with just the engine creates a situation where pitching might occur. The only way to counter this was to create negative lift on the tail and to position the internal weight further aft. During operating speeds and during landing, the weight needs to be replaced toward the rear of the plane to compensate for the burn off of the fuel.

"We also installed and designed the plane around the new Pratt and Whitney WASP 425-horsepower engine. The nine cylinders and 1,340-cubic-inch displacement engine weighs only six hundred and fifty pounds.

"It's the same engine that was used by Lindbergh. During the five years of being in service, the engine has proven not only to be extremely fast but totally reliable for a long trip. Take care of the engine and it will take care of you."

"I can't thank you enough. It's more than I could have expected," Clyde says.

Clyde looks inside the plane. "Where are the seats and controls?"

Giuseppe laughs and says, "You said you wanted it light."

"We thought it would have seats," Clyde says, worried.

"Don't worry. We are customizing the seats to make them lighter. You'll be able to take delivery of the plane next week."

Chapter 9

A Month Later
In the Hangar

Clyde is preparing *Miss Veedol* in a private hangar when Hugh comes blasting in.

"Clyde, look at this. The round-the-world record of the Graf Zeppelin was just broken." He shoves a newspaper into Clyde's face.

"We can break that record?" Clyde asks.

"Wiley Post and Harold Gatty *shattered* the old record. The new record is eight days, fifteen hours, and fifty-one minutes, smashing the old record of twenty days," Hugh says.

"Their plane is faster. Our route will allow us to make less stops. By the way, where have you been?" Clyde says.

"I have some legal mumbo jumbo for you to sign," he answers.

Clyde says, "What is it this time?"

Hugh gives him the papers. "Something about endorsements," he lies. He knows Clyde will not be agreeable if he looks too closely at what his attorneys had drawn up.

Clyde takes a quick look and signs the papers, then hands them back to Hugh.

"I haven't seen you for a few weeks," Clyde says, curious. "What have you been up to?"

"I got married to Mary Ellen," he answers, smiling wide.

"Well, congratulations. No wonder you have been preoccupied."

Clyde is obviously a little put-off since he didn't even know about the wedding or where Hugh had been for the few weeks. His mind races, thinking he wasn't good enough for the high-society folks to invite him.

Seeing Clyde is a bit upset, Hugh replies, "We kept the wedding really small. She is worried about the trip and wanted to get married before we took off."

"Congratulations again. I need to go home for a few days as well to see my mother and girlfriend before we leave."

Hugh has been gone for so long that he is not sure what the final plan is.

"When are we leaving?" he asks.

"I'm figuring we'll leave July twenty-ninth from Roosevelt Field on Long Island."

Chapter 10

The Flight

Roosevelt Field
Long Island, New York

Crowds of people and media personnel are at the field. Hugh and Clyde are looking around, taking it all in, and Hugh goes to look over the edge of the airfield. The airfield is only about three miles from the shoreline.

Hugh asks, "Since the plane is carrying so much fuel, what happens if we aren't airborne before we run out of runway?"

"See that dark spot down on the field below?" Clyde responds.

Hugh looks down to the field again and sees the place Clyde is talking about. "Yes."

"Remember Rene, the French flier? This is where he died," Clyde answers.

Hugh winces. "That is not very reassuring."

They walk back to the plane. Hugh's wife, Mary Ellen, and his mother, Alice, are there.

Hugh looks around and realizes he doesn't see Diane there. "Where is Diane?"

Clyde shrugs and says matter-of-factly, "She said she didn't want to watch."

Mary Ellen goes up to *Miss Veedol* and gives Hugh a lingering kiss. "I will be missing you, darling. Good luck."

"I will miss you too. I will be home before you know it," he says.

"Bon voyage," Alice says to the men.

Hugh thanks his mother for her help and gives her a hug.

Alice watches her son walk over to the plane for the final preflight check. "Just be careful, Son."

Clyde looks out at the spectators. He spots a familiar face in the crowd. He walks over and straight up to Diane.

"Hi," he says, grinning.

Diane blushes a little bit as she says, "Hello."

"I'm happy you were able to get off work after all. I didn't want to leave without seeing you," he says.

She looks down at her hands clasped in her lap. "Yes, I wanted to be here."

"I thought you didn't want to see me take off."

"I don't. This is really hard for me."

He promises her that he'll be fine.

Diane says, "And what if you crash?"

"It's best not to think about it," he says.

She doesn't say anything but gives him a big hug. The crowd sees all of this going on, and they clap.

Clyde looks up at the crowd and gives them a goofy smile. "I guess I've got to be going."

Diane looks at him and says, "I love you, Clyde." There are tears forming in her eyes.

Maybe for the first time in his life he thinks he is in love too.

She tells him, "I can't stand the thought of losing you."

"I love you too, Diane. You will see. I'll be fine." They share a lingering kiss and embrace. "I'll be back." Clyde turns around, walks back, and boards the plane.

The ground crew turns the engine propeller of the plane to get it started. Smoke bellows out the exhaust as the pistons come to life. Another member of the ground crew pulls the chock from under the wheel. The plane lumbers down runway one.

Clyde turns to Hugh and says, "This is it!"

"Pretty exciting!"

The plane roars down the runway, but it is obvious the overfilled plane isn't going to make it.

Clyde yells, "Pull the dump valve."

"Now?"

"This would be a good time."

Miss Veedol flies over the edge and drops as hundreds of gallons of fuel are dumped. The plane gains altitude and comes back around for a landing.

Clyde breathes an audible sigh of relief. "That was close!"

Hugh's heart is racing. "I thought we might see Davy Jones's locker today," he says, laughing nervously.

While the plane is being refueled, the crowd grows impatient.

"We're going to try this on the longer runway number two," Clyde tells Hugh.

"The other runway was a little scary," Hugh says.

The plane is started. The engines revved. The plane begins to lumber down the clay-packed runway. *Miss Veedol* picks up speed and gradually lifts off into the low-lying clouds.

Clyde says, "We are going to have to change our route somewhat."

Worried, Hugh asks, "Why?"

"The southern route is a little longer, but we should be able to avoid some inclement weather."

Hugh says, "I can't even see the ocean!"

Clyde shakes his head. "I don't think we'll see any ocean."

Several hours later, Hugh looks a little pale. *Miss Veedol* is bouncing around in some turbulence.

"Hugh, are you all right?" asks Clyde.

"I really need a cigarette."

"It's a bad habit. We are going to fourteen thousand feet. The air should be a little smoother there."

Hugh decides he may make it through the flight easier if he tries to sleep. When he wakes, he glances out the window and asks, "How far have we gone?"

"We've been in the air for about ten hours. Do you mind taking over the controls for a couple hours while I try to get some rest?"

"Sure."

"Thanks. Just keep the plane on course."

As Clyde wakes, he sees there is nothing visible except the clouds and fog below them.

Clyde takes over the controls again as *Miss Veedol* continues across the Atlantic for another twenty hours. Clyde and Hugh take turns flying and resting throughout the flight.

"I'll take over now. We are getting close to land," Clyde says.

Hugh looks at him. "How can you tell?"

"You just know."

Clyde checks the charts. "As a matter of fact, we are over Ireland, headed over Saint George's Channel. We should be at Croydon, London in a couple hours."

Chapter 11

London, England

A couple hours later, they land at Croydon Airport just outside London. A small group of people meet them as they land.

An aviator with a stopwatch meets them as they are disembarking from the plane. "Congratulations! You both just qualified for the fifth nonstop Atlantic flight in history."

Clyde remarks, "We took the southern route since the weather was not good."

"In that case, your flight was the first successful flight across the Atlantic using this longer route. Truly remarkable," the aviator says, grinning.

"What was our time? We are attempting to break the round-the-world record," Clyde says.

"You are a few hours off Gatty's time at this point in the trip."

As they are refueling and doing the final preflight check of the plane, a Bentley sedan pulls onto the airfield and drives up to *Miss Veedol*. Hugh's cousin Thomas jumps out of the sedan.

"Hugh! Your mother told us you would be landing here. She said you got married. Congratulations!"

"Fancy meeting you here, Thomas," replies Hugh.

"Jump in. We're going to get a quick bite. We've got a little get-together planned." Hugh runs over to the sedan.

He stops before getting into the car and yells to Clyde, "These are some relatives. We'll see you shortly."

Clyde asks, "Where are you going?"

"They have arranged a small celebration. We'll be back soon," says Hugh.

"How did they know we were landing here?" Clyde asks.

"My mother cabled them to let them know we should be arriving."

"Hugh, have you forgotten that we are trying to beat a record? We need to take off for the next leg of the trip soon."

"We'll be back soon. They want to celebrate my marriage." Hugh jumps into the sedan and off they go.

"I hear you are up to no good," Thomas says, chuckling, as soon as Hugh shuts the car door.

Hugh turns to his cousin in the backseat of the Bentley. Smiling, he says, "Oh, Thomas, it is good. It is very good."

He looks out the window, watching London go by, and continues, "My attorneys have written up a very rigid contract that will impose a gag order on *Pangborn* for one year if we complete this flight."

"Why would you not want him to talk about the flight? If you break the record, it will be an absolutely historic event."

"He'll be silenced, but I won't. Clyde will just be a footnote in the history books. Not to mention, any money awarded will go to my family."

"You actually got him to sign this?" Thomas asks, unbelieving.

"He would have signed just about anything to get the financial backing. I just handed him the papers. He barely even looked at them."

Thomas nods and turns to stare out the window. "Sounds like you haven't changed much, Cousin."

Several hours later, Clyde is waiting with a group of aviators and airport staff.

One of the aviators asks, "What are you going to do if he doesn't return shortly? You're running behind schedule. It's almost 2:30 in the afternoon already!"

"I suppose that I have to keep going if I want to have any chance of breaking the record. Do you mind giving me a jump?"

At that, the aviator nods, and the two of them walk out to *Miss Veedol*. The aviator gives the engine a jump, and it fires up. As Clyde waves the man off, the Bentley returns. Hugh jumps out and waves goodbye to his relatives. He runs over to the plane and takes his place.

Inside the cockpit, Hugh asks, "Where were you going?"

"Off to Berlin. Oh, I hope you had a nice visit."

"I did. I thought you might be upset."

Clyde smirks. "Not really. We were only *several* hours behind Post and Gatty's schedule when we landed."

Chapter 12

Tempelhof Airport
Berlin, Germany

Miss Veedol arrives in Germany about five hours later. A ground crew comes out to direct the plane, and once the plane has come to a stop, Clyde tells the crew to refuel the plane.

A member of the ground crew says in a thick German accent, "They are expecting you, Mr. Pangborn." He escorts Clyde and Hugh to an area of the airport where several German officers in Nazi uniforms are waiting and a formal dinner has been prepared.

"We were expecting you. We figured you would be hungry. The table is beautiful, don't you think?" an officer says to them.

Clyde thanks them for their hospitality, and the officer continues, "Where are you flying to from here?"

Clyde tells him they will be flying to Moscow.

"Careful in Russia," the officer responds.

After the dinner, a small group assembles to see them off. The German officers salute and say, "Heil Hitler," as the plane taxis down the runway and takes off.

When they are in the air and the plane is safely at cruising altitude, Clyde tells Hugh, "I have to rest for a few hours. The course is set to Moscow. You need to stay on it. Wake me up in a few hours."

"Ok. I feel pretty good. You get some rest," Hugh says.

"I would hope so."

Several hours later, the plane is bucking up and down, and Clyde wakes up.

He looks around and says, "What is going on, Hugh?"

"I didn't want to wake you. We're in the middle of a storm."

Clyde figures out their coordinates. "We are a little off our route."

"How far?"

"About one hour. We'll set it down it Moscow and refuel. We can still break the record. We have about five hours until we reach Moscow."

Hugh says, "Maybe I should rest now?"

"That's a good idea. When we leave Moscow, you'll fly for a while and I'll rest again then."

Chapter 13

Moscow, Russia

When they arrive at the airport in Moscow, it is morning and rain is pouring down. The airstrip is covered with several inches of water.

"Hugh, when we leave Moscow, you have to be really careful. We are going to cross the Ural Mountains. Be certain to stay above ten thousand feet. We have a twenty-hour flight to Novosibirsk."

After a short stopover in Moscow, they are on their way again. Over Siberia they encounter a ferocious rainstorm. The airplane is tossed about vertically and laterally, and they are forced to try to land.

Clyde shouts over the noise of the engine and the storm, "We have to set it down, Hugh."

"We can't set it down."

"We don't have any choice. I need you to look for a runway, Hugh."

Hugh searches the map. "I think there is a small airport."

Clyde looks at the map to be sure and says, "Perfect! Khabarovsk, Siberia. We are about fifteen miles away."

Hugh looks out the window. "I think the runway is just below us. I see the control tower, but the runway looks like it is just a muddy lake."

"There it is. We have to set it down," Clyde says.

Miss Veedol comes in for a landing. There is almost no visibility. The plane is dropping just over the barren wasteland when the dirt airstrip becomes visible.

Hugh looks out the window and sees a muddy patch submerged in water.

"That's not an airstrip," he says.

Clyde shouts, "I'm setting her down. Prepare for landing." The Bellanca J-300 slides off the runway and becomes bogged down. There is no way the plane will be able to take off again.

Clyde is devastated. "We are finished. We won't break the record."

"I can't believe it. That's it? All that planning and money." He hangs his head.

"We didn't have any choice. And we were already behind schedule."

"How far are we behind?" asks Hugh.

"We are about twenty-seven hours behind the record."

"Is it possible to make up the time?"

"We are out of the race to beat Gatty's record. We can't make up twenty-seven hours."

"Out of the race? There's no way we cannot win."

Instead of being upset with Hugh for being too dense to understand and setting them back several hours, Clyde says, "I do have another idea that could make this trip worth our while. Before we left, I read about a prize being offered for the first nonstop flight across the Pacific."

"Across the Pacific nonstop? We aren't prepared for a nonstop Pacific flight."

"We will be. Besides, I believe it will be easier than the round-the-world flight we were attempting."

"Why?" Hugh asks.

"I don't have to worry about you running off with relatives at every stop."

Hugh laughs. "Very funny, Clyde."

Chapter 14

Khabarovsk, Russia

Several hundred locals greet Hugh and Clyde in Khabarovsk, Russia, when they see the plane land at the airport. The locals pull the airplane into the shelter area. Hugh and Clyde disembark, happy to stretch their legs but heartbroken they will not break the record.

As they decide what to do, Hugh plays cards with the locals, and he is rather good at it.

"All this time and money and now we are quitting," Hugh says without looking up from his cards.

"I have researched the issue and several attempts have been made to cross the Pacific. No one has gotten close to doing it."

"There is a reason no one has done it. It is impossible. Lindbergh's nonstop flight across the Atlantic was three thousand miles. How long is the Pacific?"

"About forty-five hundred miles. Lindbergh's flight was over thirty hours. Our flight will be over forty hours. Of course, I will have you to help me."

Hugh laughs. "Clyde, it's impossible. We can't do it. I won't do it. The reason no one has done it is that is it impossible."

Clyde tells Hugh that they should qualify for the Japanese *Asahi Shimbun* newspaper prize of fifty thousand dollars if they can do it.

This seems to gain Hugh's attention. "Fifty thousand dollars?"

Clyde has to add the disclaimer in case they don't make it. "Of course, Hugh, the six earlier attempts all ended in disaster."

"That's it, Clyde. I quit. We couldn't navigate across Europe together. How are we going to get across the Pacific?"

"Think of Europe as a trial run. This will be the real deal," Clyde says, wanting to encourage Hugh.

Hugh is apprehensive and says, "Europe didn't go so well. I don't know if I want to do this."

"Listen, the first nonstop Pacific attempt was made in 1930 with the Bromley-Gatty team. Their plane had a range of four thousand miles. They took off from Sabishiro north of Tokyo and flew 1,250 miles, mostly in clouds and headwinds. They realized they wouldn't make it and flew back to Japan.

"The next attempt was a Japanese guy named Yoshihara. He flew one thousand miles in a Junkers open cockpit, and the engine stopped over the Dragon's Triangle. The plane had floats, and a passing ship picked him up several hours later."

"Talk about luck," Hugh says.

"I know it. Then a barnstormer named Reginald Robbins tried in a Lockheed Vega that was to be refueled in the air. That didn't work, and that plane went down over the Dragon's Triangle."

"What's the Dragon's Triangle?"

"It's an area in the ocean off the coast of Japan where boats and planes just disappear. There is no explanation."

"Is that true?" Hugh asks, puzzled.

Clyde smiles. "Of course, it's possible. The Japanese are sometimes a little superstitious. There is more. There were several more attempts. One guy failed to get off the sands at Sabishiro and crashed into the sea."

"I'm not doing it. I'll figure out another way to get home," Hugh says.

Clyde is not going to let Hugh get out of this so easily. "Hugh, it's possible. Think how huge it would be if we were the ones to actually do it! Besides, we have to go that way to get home. Charles

Smith tried in 1928 in a Fokker. He did an island-hopping flight from Oakland to Brisbane. It wasn't nonstop but he proved the trip is possible.

"It is only fifteen hundred miles longer than what Lindbergh flew when he crossed the Atlantic in his Ryan NYP. This should be a breeze."

"You are crazy, Clyde. We won't make it. The plane wasn't designed for it."

"We have to take off from Japan anyway to get home. Let's look at a place to launch. I have studied this, Hugh. It is possible."

A while later, they are still in Siberia and rain hasn't stopped. While the plane is still bogged down in the mud and unable to take off, Clyde works to plan the next round of their trip.

Hugh asks, "What is our plan now?"

"I have to contact the US Embassy in Japan. They will contact the Japanese Aviation Bureau to get flight approval. One we get the approval, we'll depart for Tachikawa airport near Tokyo," Clyde answers.

"Sounds complicated."

Clyde laughs. "Not really. The embassy should be able to help us."

On the phone, Clyde says, "Yes, operator, this is Clyde Pangborn and Hugh Herndon. I cabled the editor of the Japanese *Times* and requested that the American embassy obtain landing permission from the Japanese Aviation Bureau. Yes. Thanks for taking my call. You haven't heard anything yet? OK, I'll let Hugh know that his mother called."

Several days later, the airfield at Khabarovsk has partially dried out. Grey clouds linger but it isn't raining.

"Not a word from the US Embassy. We had better take off before the rains return," Clyde says to Hugh.

Hugh asks, "Do we have clearance?"

"The US Embassy should obtain landing approval at Tachikawa."

"What if they think we are the Chinese or something and shoot us out of the sky?"

Clyde laughs. "Hugh, that is the most intellectual thing I have ever heard you say."

Hugh joins in the laughter and says, "Slip of the tongue."

After flying across the Atlantic and landing in muddy airstrips, *Miss Veedol* is looking a little tattered. The tires are covered with mud. A small group of people watch as Hugh and Clyde taxi down the muddy field and take off.

Chapter 15

Japan

From the airplane, Hugh takes pictures of Mount Fuji while Clyde flies. They are amazed by the beauty of Japan.

They accidently fly into restricted Japanese airspace over secret military facilities.

When Japanese Intelligence spots the plane in restricted airspace, an intelligence officer says, "Commander, unidentified plane is crossing into restricted airspace."

The commander asks, "Have you tried to contact the plane?"

"We have tried all channels. There is no response."

"Shoot it down!" the commander orders.

Explosions erupt all around the plane as the Japanese begin shooting. Clyde turns the plane into a steep dive away from where the shooting is coming from.

Hugh says, "Now we're in for it." The men are visibly shaken, but Clyde tries to keep a clear head.

"As long as they don't shoot us down, we'll be fine. I guess this is our message that we didn't obtain clearance yet. Tachikawa Airfield is an hour away. We'll land there."

Chapter 16

Tachikawa Airfield
Tokyo, Japan

Miss Veedol circles around and lands, then taxis to the side of the runway. Angry Japanese officials and guards run toward and surround the plane with weapons drawn.

They shout orders in Japanese, instructing Clyde and Hugh to get out of the plane.

As Clyde and Hugh make their way out of the plane, an official yells at them in Japanese, "Where are your landing papers?" Neither of the aviators understand Japanese.

Clyde answers, "We are American citizens. We don't have a flight permit with us. We assumed the US Embassy arranged it." He turns to Hugh. "Hold your hands up so they see you don't have a weapon."

Hugh asks, "What did they say?"

Clyde shrugs. "I have no idea."

"I take it we didn't get our clearance."

The guards escort them to a private room at the airfield where they wait. There is a guard inside the room and a guard stationed outside the door.

A Japanese interpreter walks into the room with a pad and paper and four armed guards. He sits down across the table from Clyde and Hugh.

The interpreter asks them what their names are.

"My name is Clyde Pangborn. I'm an American citizen. I demand that I have an attorney present during questioning."

The interpreter turns to Hugh who says, "My name is Hugh Herndon, and I demand the use of a telephone."

"You are not in a position to make demands. You are both under arrest for espionage."

Clyde gasps and says, "Espionage?"

"You flew over a fortified military facility. We found the cameras in your plane. You were taking pictures of our military installations. You have no flight papers and no flight plan."

"Our landing was supposed to be cleared by the US Embassy," Clyde says.

The interpreter is not relenting and tells the men, "I do not know why you were flying over our military installations taking photos. I only know that you did it."

The four guards grab Clyde's and Hugh's arms and take them out to the waiting bus.

Chapter 17

The Black Dragon Society

Uchida Ryohei founded the Japanese nationalist group Kokuryukai, later known as the Black Dragon Society, in 1901.

In Japanese, fifty-year-old Uchida tells his men that two American fliers were caught flying over and photographing military installations.

A Japanese government official tells him the US Embassy is attempting to provide documents for them to leave.

Uchida tells the official, "They are American. They must suspect our plans for Manchuria."

"The Americans have been put under house arrest, and they will be tried for treason. The judge in the case is evaluating the evidence."

Imperial Hotel
Tokyo, Japan

Two military guards escort Clyde and Hugh inside the hotel, which was designed by Frank Lloyd Wright, where they are to stay while they are under house arrest.

Hugh looks around. "This is the prison?"

"I can't tell if we are guests or prisoners," Clyde says.

The two guards escort them to their rooms at the hotel where guards have been posted outside their doors.

Clyde says, "See you in the morning, Hugh."

"Yeah, it will be nice to actually get some sleep. Wonder if I can get some cigarettes?" Hugh says.

"Can't hurt to ask." Clyde laughs.

Several hours later, there is a knock on Clyde's door, and he opens it to find a twenty-something Japanese woman wearing military-style fatigues.

In perfect English, she says, "Here are your cigarettes," and hands him a pack from an ornate tray.

Clyde smiles as he says, "Domo arigato. I don't smoke. They must be for my partner."

She nods and says, "My name is Yumiko. I will be your food server while you are here." Clyde bows his head slightly.

"Your English is perfect."

"I lived for a few years in America."

"Splendid. Where did you live?" Clyde asks.

"I went to school at Washington State and received my degree at the University of Washington in nutrition." She pauses for a moment, suddenly realizing he is probably Pangborn the flier. "Are you the aviator Clyde Pangborn?"

When Clyde tells her he is, Yumiko says, "My father has read about you. I think he would like to meet you."

"He would like to meet *me*?"

"Yes. He read about your attempt to break the round-the-world record."

Clyde tells Yumiko that he is looking forward to meeting her father.

Yumiko replies, "I have to go."

"It was nice to meet you. My partner, Hugh, is in the next room."

"It was nice to meet you too. Thank you."

The next day, there is a knock at Clyde's door.

Clyde opens it, sees Yumiko, and says, "Hello."

Yumiko smiles. "Your partner is much different from you. He thought I brought him more than just cigarettes."

Clyde laughs. "Oh, you noticed."

Yumiko smiles again.

"Who makes the food?" asks Clyde.

"I prepare the meals. Are they satisfactory?" says Yumiko.

"They are incredible."

"I have brought you lunch, but I have to go now. I'll see you later in the evening."

Clyde can't help but notice that Yumiko is rather attractive. He thinks of Diane, and he misses the companionship that they shared. He knows that she will be waiting for him when he returns. However, he innocently wants to ask if Yumiko would like to stay just to share some conversation. He would love to hear about their customs and culture and how the Depression has affected Japan. He realizes that he is in a society that very few people from the West have had an opportunity to visit. He decides to take the chance. "Would you stay for a cup of coffee or tea?"

Yumiko replies, "I am unable right now, but I will be back later."

Later that evening, Yumiko walks in and closes the door behind her.

"Thank you for coming back," Clyde says.

"Shh. I am making a plan for you to visit my father."

"What do you mean visit your father?"

"He thinks you and he should meet. By his calculations, you will never complete your journey."

"He is correct. The plane requires extensive modifications. How does he know this?"

"He is an engineer," Yumiko responds.

"Does he know where our plane is?"

"The authorities locked it up in a hangar at the airport."

"I can't leave here. In case you have forgotten, I am a prisoner."

"I have to go now. I will return"

Yumiko leaves the room and the guards move aside.

Later in the evening, there is a tapping on Clyde's window. Clyde pulls the panel to the side and sees Yumiko and her father outside. Clyde opens up the window.

Clyde whispers, "Yumiko."

"Meet my father, Yosh."

Yumiko's father, wearing traditional Japanese garments, bows his head. Clyde bows to Yumiko's father and says, "Please, come in."

Yosh comes in with Yumiko.

After a few silent moments, Clyde says, "Sorry, please sit down."

Yosh and Yumiko take a seat on the sofa.

"Does your father speak English?"

Yumiko and her father speak a few words in Japanese, and she says, "My father speaks English, but he asks for you to speak slowly since he hasn't spoken English for many years. He said to call him Yosh."

"A pleasure to meet you, Mr. Yosh," replies Clyde.

"Yosh. Not Mr. Yosh, Mr. Pangborn," Yosh says.

"Please call me Clyde."

"I located your plane in a hangar earlier this evening."

"How did you do that?"

Yosh smiles and says, "I picked the locked door. Easy."

Clyde says, "Is the plane all right?"

"All right for local flying. Not for flight across the Pacific. Lots of work to do."

Clyde runs a hand through his hair and exhales heavily. "How can we do this?"

"We work at night."

"It seems risky," Clyde says.

"Not risky as long as you don't get caught," jokes Yosh.

Clyde was caught off guard because the comment was so unlike what he thought the Japanese represented culturally. He smiles. "That makes sense."

As Yosh stands, he says, "One more thing. There is a group called the Black Dragons. They want the Japanese to be first to fly across the Pacific. They may try to keep you from making your flight."

Clyde is worried. "Black Dragons. Are they dangerous?"

"Not dangerous and as long as you don't get caught?" Yosh says, laughing.

Yosh is tickled by his own joke and can't stop laughing. His laughter is contagious and Clyde laughs with him. Several minutes later, the grown men get a hold of themselves. Clyde tells Yosh that they should go before they are caught. After Yosh and Yumiko leave, Clyde knocks on the wall between his room and Hugh's.

Clyde calls, "Hugh."

"What is it? It's the middle of the night," Hugh says, irritation apparent in his voice.

"We really need to work on the airplane. Our plan to cross the Pacific is not possible without modifications."

"We are locked up," says Hugh.

"Yumiko and her father were just here. They can help us."

Hugh isn't buying it. "Sounds like a trap."

"They are all that we have."

"I am nervous about this."

"There really isn't any other way. If they let us go and the plane isn't ready, we will crash. Simple as that."

The next morning, Yumiko arrives to the room with a breakfast tray.

Clyde says, "Good morning."

Yumiko replies, "I brought you an American-style breakfast."

"For me?"

"I thought you might enjoy bacon and eggs. I also brought you some news. My father would like to meet tonight at the hangar."

Clyde tells her that he is concerned. He doesn't want to put her at risk.

"My father and I have discussed the risk. He believes this is the opportunity of his lifetime to do something great. He believes strongly in your journey across the Pacific."

Clyde is surprised that this is so important to Yosh too.

"My father will meet you at the hangar at 11:00 tonight. I will bring flashlights later and escort you to the hangar."

"I don't know how to thank you enough. Please, just be careful," Clyde says, overjoyed to be receiving help.

Yumiko, dressed in black, comes by the hotel later and lightly taps on Clyde's window. He opens the window but doesn't turn on the light. She tells Clyde to meet at the hotel arboretum.

Clyde taps on the wall. Hugh taps back. They both climb out their windows and meet Yumiko at the hotel arboretum.

Behind the arboretum is a trail leading to the airstrip. The airfield's perimeter is adjacent to the town. Yumiko gives Clyde and Hugh flashlights and tells them to follow her.

As they follow the trail to the airstrip, Hugh breaks the silence, whispering to Clyde that he thinks Yumiko fancies him.

Clyde whispers, "Why do you say that?"

Hugh matter-of-factly says, "If they don't go for me, it means there is someone else."

Clyde says, "Could be anyone else."

Hugh whispers, "You just haven't noticed, buddy. She suddenly shines when she is near you. You don't see the way she looks at you?"

Clyde tells Hugh that he really doesn't see it like that.

"Let me put it like this. If she didn't like you, there would be no reason for her to do this. I would think that we were being set up."

"That makes sense."

"What is going on with Diane?" Hugh asks.

"Gotta see what happens when we get home."

"Remember: any port in a storm."

Clyde tells him, "We need to keep quiet."

The lights of the airfield shine in the background, and they arrive at the hangar. Yumiko had gotten a bit ahead of them, so they couldn't find her in the darkness, and Yosh did not seem to have arrived yet.

"Looks like we are early," Hugh says.

"Let's just wait here." At that moment, out of the darkness, Yumiko comes up and taps Clyde on the shoulder.

Yumiko puts a finger to her lips. "My father is here. He is opening up the lock on the hangar door."

They walk around the hangar where Yosh is silently picking the lock.

"There. Got it. Easy," says Yosh as he steps back into the darkness.

Yumiko is concerned about being outside where someone could hear them and motions for Hugh and Clyde to follow her inside the hangar.

"This whole thing is a little creepy," Hugh says.

The door closes behind them, and Yosh turns on a light.

"Hugh, this is my father," Yumiko says.

"Sure he isn't British Secret Service?" Hugh asks.

Yumiko gives Hugh a bewildered look.

Hugh says, "Just a joke."

Yosh laughs. "Ha! I got it. You funny guy. Me secret agent."

Hugh laughs and holds his hand out. "My name is Hugh."

Yosh doesn't take his hand but makes a little bow.

"My name is Yosh."

Miss Veedol sits in the middle of the hangar. Yosh looks at the plane and says, "I didn't realize the plane was so large."

"She was custom built for us. There are many innovations such as the aerodynamic struts. There is no starter to reduce the weight. The fuel tanks are larger than normal for greater distance," Clyde says. "At least she has wings" says Yosh and he laughs again.

Chapter 18

The Hangar

Every night, Clyde and Hugh leave the hotel at 10:00 p.m. to meet Yosh and Yumiko, and they work all night until 4:00 a.m.

Yosh says, "I hear something."

Hugh quickly puts out his cigarette, and Clyde turns off the light. All four listen for a moment and hear voices outside the hangar.

They all quietly go to a back parts room and pull the door closed.

A moment later, several security police enter the hangar and turn on the lights.

One of the officers says, "It looks like someone has been in here."

Another policeman agrees and says he smells smoke.

They look around the hangar but don't see anyone. They try the door to the parts room, but it is locked. "Some neighborhood kids must have gotten in," one says, and they lock up the hangar.

After the airport police leave, Clyde and the others agree they had better leave in case the police call someone else to investigate.

"We should wait several days before we meet again. Hurry back to the hotel," Yosh says.

Hugh and Clyde hurry back along the trail in the full moon and return to the hotel.

Chapter 19

Imperial Hotel

Clyde slides open the window, leaps into bed, and pulls the covers over him.

A minute later, a security guard barges into the room, turning on the light.

Clyde pretends he is sleeping and has just been woken up.

The guard looks around the room and sees that everything is all right. The guards go to Hugh's room, and he is also sleeping soundly in bed.

The guards tap Hugh's bed with a nightstick. Hugh opens his eyes, and the guards turn off the light and leave the room.

Several days later, when Yumiko serves Clyde lunch, she says, "My father says tonight we continue. He said to meet at 11:30. He will be at the hangar earlier to check for guards."

Later that night, Yosh meets Hugh and Clyde outside the hangar.

Yosh says, "Hugh, you maintain the watch. We will switch with you in a few hours."

Clyde turns to him and says, "If you see anything suspicious or hear anyone approaching the hangar, let me know."

Hugh nods and stays outside while the others go inside the hangar.

"You and Hugh are getting lots of press in the newspaper," Yosh tells Clyde as he enters the hangar. "The Black Dragon Society is a far-right organization. They want your plane confiscated. They do not want you released. They believe only a Japanese plane with a Japanese crew should conquer the dragon."

Clyde asks, "What is so frightening about *the dragon*?"

"Legend says the Pacific can't be conquered. Many boats have just disappeared in an area off the coast of Tokyo."

"That is just an old legend."

Perhaps Yosh replies. However, I have spoken to people who have been in triangle and survived. It is real. Yosh hands papers to Clyde. "What do you think of these drawings for the plane?"

Clyde studies the drawings and says, "These modifications are excellent. I have a few minor changes though."

Yosh says, "I can have a few of these parts fabricated."

"The landing gear needs to be disassembled so we can fabricate the bolts."

"We need to make it look like no one has tampered with the plane in case the authorities inspect it and the hangar."

"Ok. We need to install additional fuel tanks. I believe there is an area under the floorboard. We also need to add additional oil capacity."

"The time is now. If you are released, the government will demand that you leave Japan immediately," says Yosh.

Later, Clyde and Yosh are fitting the extra fuel tanks under the floorboard. Clyde asks Yosh if the tanks were tested, and Yosh assures him the tanks were tested after they were manufactured.

"They should be all right. We will have to take off with the heaviest fuel load in the wing ever attempted in a Bellanca."

Yosh chuckles. "I hope it flies." Yosh keeps laughing and says, "Me funny guy."

Clyde isn't quite so flippant and smirks at Yosh. "Me too. I was going to ask you, what do you think about jettisoning the landing gear during flight?"

"Jettisoning? Like getting rid of?"

Clyde laughs. "Yes."

Yosh asks, "Then how do you land?"

"We land on the protected fuselage of the plane."

Yosh thinks for a moment, and he immediately sees the sense in it. "You won't have the extra weight of the 500-pound landing gear. But it seems risky to land on the belly of the plane. Has it been done before?" he asks.

"Several years ago, an Australian named Harry Hawker made an unsuccessful attempt to cross the Atlantic. He designed a way to remove the landing gear in flight, using a series of clips and springs attached to a cable. By pulling on the cable after takeoff, the whole landing gear structure fell away."

Yosh realizes the genius in the theory and wants to figure out how to design it. "Great idea. We can do it. Makes the plane more aerodynamic."

"We need to design a steel skid plate to protect the fuselage."

"Has to be light. Maybe aluminum?" Yosh says.

"With the added fuel, the plane might not have enough range to make the forty-five hundred mile crossing unless we do this. According to my calculations, we should gain fifteen miles per hour airspeed, and that would give us an few extra hundred miles additional range."

Yosh is on a mission. "I will see what materials I can get without raising suspicion."

Yumiko is happy her father is pleased with a man that she likes. She was interested in a couple of Japanese men before, but her father never seemed to like them. It is obvious that Clyde and her father have a lot in common. "You two are always chattering," she tells them.

Yosh asks Clyde, "What does she mean by chattering? It's a new word for me."

"She means that we talk a lot!" Clyde says, laughing.

Yosh laughs with him and says, "Ha, she funny girl! I think she likes you."

Clyde smiles. "I think I like her too."

The next morning at the Imperial Hotel, Yumiko brings Clyde an early breakfast. When she walks in, she stomps across the room to set the tray on the table. "Here's your breakfast," she says.

"You seem upset," Clyde says.

"I am not upset," she snaps.

"Yes, you are. I am sure of it."

"No, I'm not," she says.

Clyde knows something is different because her eyes sparkled for a moment. That gentle sparkle was barely a glimpse into her soul, but it was there, and there was no way she could hide it. "I can see it in your eyes. Your eyes are flickering like beautiful Baltic amber."

Yumiko knows she has given him access to a part of herself she didn't know existed. He didn't have to say anything but he saw it. "You are mistaken. I have to go," she says. She picks up the tray from the previous night and goes to leave the room.

Clyde grabs Yumiko around the waist and laughs.

"Leave me alone," she says as he turns her around.

Clyde meets her gaze and says, "Sorry, I was taken by you the moment I met you."

"Then why do you talk to my father all the time?"

"I like your father. He is a really special man."

"He really likes you too. He is trying to protect me."

"Protect you from what?"

Yumiko shrugs. "He knows how I feel about you too. He wants to keep you safe."

"How would he know how you feel about me?"

Yumiko says, "Fathers know."

"Know what?"

"You speak too much," she says.

With that, Yumiko goes to kiss him, forgetting she is holding a tray. They tip the food tray over and the dishes make a crashing noise.

From outside the door, the guard asks in Japanese, "You all right?"

Yumiko answers, "Yes!"

She gives Clyde a quick kiss, picks up the dishes, and goes to the door. She stops and turns to him. Smiling, she says, "See you tonight!"

Three weeks pass, and the modifications take shape. Clyde and Yosh enjoy talking with each other as they work in the hangar.

"I haven't seen Yumiko for several days," Clyde says.

"Yumiko likes you. She is sad you are leaving."

"Nah."

"Yes, fathers know. Her eyes sparkle when she sees you."

"I see that too. I thought she was mad with me."

Yosh laughs. "Yeah, mad in love."

On September 18, 1931, the Japanese invade Manchuria in China. Yosh takes an English newspaper off the counter and hands it to Clyde. Clyde reads the headline aloud, "Japan invades Manchuria."

"It is important that we complete the modifications to the plane. We are now at war with China."

"Do you think that we are ready?" Clyde asks.

"I don't know. We need to obtain at least ninety miles per hour for takeoff speed. The plane is fifty percent overweight. I don't know if the tires will even hold up during takeoff. And I don't know if the wings will hold up. Aside from that, you are good to go."

Later, back at the Imperial Hotel, Yumiko tells Clyde, "Japan invaded Manchuria yesterday. We are at war with China."

"Your father told me. This looks bad for us leaving Japan."

Yumiko says, "I heard some officials speaking yesterday. They want to get your case to trial right away."

"The plane is ready."

"You are due in court tomorrow," she says reluctantly.

Chapter 20

Tokyo District Court

The Japanese attorney appointed to Hugh and Clyde by the US Embassy greets them at the courthouse. "Good afternoon, gentlemen. I'll get right to it—I have bad news. You will most likely be found guilty."

Clyde and Hugh balk. "Why do you think we will be found guilty?" Clyde asks.

"Statistically, ninety-nine percent of defendants in the Japanese system are found guilty. That is the way the system is structured. Do you have any questions?"

"How could we be guilty of espionage? We haven't done anything," Hugh says.

"You are both protected from self-incrimination and from hearsay evidence. I have examined the evidence."

"What evidence?" Hugh asks.

"The only evidence they have are the pictures you took flying over the military installation."

"We flew over that by accident," Clyde says.

"The flight plan was not approved. The authorities have the camera and the pictures," the attorney says.

"I was taking a picture of Mount Fugi," Hugh tells him.

The attorney continues, "If you are found guilty, you can appeal to the higher court on constitutional issues. The judge who conducts the trial is authorized to call for evidence, decide guilt, and pass sentence."

"Oh great. We're dead," Clyde says, hanging his head.

When a court staff member motions from the courtroom door, the attorney says, "The judge has called your case. Just follow me. Do not speak to the judge unless he asks you to speak."

The men follow the attorney into the courtroom and take their seats. The judge speaks in Japanese and the interpreter translates to English.

The judge tells them, "On the three counts of espionage, we have evaluated the evidence."

"The evidence?" Clyde says to the attorney after the interpreter finishes the translation.

The attorney says, "Shh."

"You both are found guilty of one charge of espionage for photographing sensitive military installations. You are both sentenced to two hundred and five days of hard labor or a fine of one thousand fifty US dollars."

The interpreter translates the judgment into English.

The judge continues, "If you choose to pay the fine, Japan's Civil Aviation Bureau has permitted you to leave Japan in your aircraft within five days. You both will not be allowed to return to Japan."

After the judge's words are translated, Hugh blurts out, "Who would want to return here?"

The interpreter says to the judge in Japanese, "He said he is sorry your honor."

The judge says to the defendants in perfect English, "And that is why you will not be permitted to return to our country."

In Japanese, the judge tells the interpreter to tell the defendants they have five days to leave Japan and pay the fine or they will be taken away to serve their sentence."

The judge gets up from the bench and leaves the courtroom.

Chapter 21

The Black Dragon Society

Uchida asks the Black Dragon members what happened with the Americans in court.

One of the Black Dragon members says, "The judge fined them and allowed them to leave Japan within five days."

"They can't be allowed to fly. We need to stop them," Uchida says.

"The plane is in a secure hangar. They take off from Tachikawa Airfield tomorrow. We believe they will fly to Sabishiro Beach to prepare the aircraft," the Black Dragon says.

"Make sure they do not leave Sabishiro successfully," Uchida orders.

"We have people on the ground already waiting."

Chapter 22

Tachikawa Airfield
Tokyo, Japan
September 29, 1931

Miss Veedol is rolled out of the hangar to prepare for flight. Yumiko and Yosh are there waiting with Clyde and Hugh as they prepare to leave.

Clyde tells Yumiko that he doesn't want to say goodbye.

"This is our destiny," she says.

"We make our destiny, Yumiko."

"This will be the last time we will see each other. The judge ruled that you can't return."

"I could appeal that part of the verdict. I could ask for permission to return to your country," he says.

"No. This is our goodbye. You either will be in jail or you leave Japan forever. In either case, it is best to say goodbye now," she says. Clyde sees tears in her eyes.

Clyde is sad, and he tries to think of a way to see her. "You are too logical. You could come with us. We have enough fuel."

"I could never leave my father. I am all that he has."

Clyde knows this is really the end. It would be foolish to have her come along and put her life in jeopardy. The chances of making the journey successfully are not favorable. "Yumiko, I love you," he says.

Yumiko wipes a tear from her eye. "Don't say anything, Clyde. I love you and I will miss you too. We just ask that you remember us."

Clyde and Yumiko give each other a long embrace. They both have tears in their eyes.

Clyde goes up to Yosh and says to him, "You are the father I never had. I will always remember you." Clyde takes a bow.

Yosh bows out of respect. "I will always remember you too."

"I hope to return to Japan someday."

Yosh replies, "Be safe, my son."

Yosh takes a long deep bow. Clyde does the same. When he turns to the plane, Hugh has already taken his seat and the engine is running.

Hugh shouts over the sound of the engine, "Come on, you lovebirds."

Clyde walks to the waiting plane glistening in the sun, and he climbs inside.

Yumiko and her father stand side by side stoically as the plane taxis and takes off down the runway.

They fly across Matsu-Wan Bay. The flight goes as scheduled, taking about two hours. Around 3:00 p.m., they land at Misawa Air Base at Sabishiro Beach about four hundred miles north of Tokyo. The plane performed beautifully.

Chapter 23

Sabishiro Beach
September 30, 1931

Miss Veedol lands and taxis to the side of the runway. Clyde and Hugh see a large crowd of people next to the runway. Clyde wonders what they are waiting for.

The crowd of people runs toward the plane.

"I think they are here for us, Clyde," Hugh says.

The mayor of Misawa comes up to the plane as Clyde and Hugh get out, and he reads aloud from a paper, "We want to welcome you to Misawa. We want to honor you with a dinner on behalf of the citizens of Misawa."

"We believe that citizens of all nations working toward an honorable goal should be hosted in friendship."

"We present you with this proclamation of friendship from the people of Misawa."

A young boy comes forward and presents five apples to Clyde.

The boy says in Japanese, "These five apples are from my family orchard. Please carry them across the ocean as a token of friendship to the people of your country."

After the interpreter translates, Clyde replies, "Thank you very much for these honors and the certificate from the people of Misawa. We would be pleased to enjoy a dinner with you this evening as we prepare the plane for our journey."

The crowd claps.

At Misawa Air Base, several Black Dragons surround the aircraft, dressed in black. The sentries don't see them.

Uchida says, "Keep an eye out. I'm going to look in the cockpit," as he climbs inside the plane.

When he climbs out of the plane, another Black Dragon asks, "Did you find the navigation maps, sir?"

Uchida grunts and shows them the maps he got from the plane.

After the dinner, Hugh is surprised to see his mother's friend Preston Finch standing next to the mayor. "Clyde, come with me," Hugh says.

Hugh holds his hand out to shake Preston's and says, "What a surprise to see you here in Japan."

"I thought I'd come in case you need a little extra help for the flight."

"An extra hand definitely won't hurt," Hugh says. "Preston Finch, meet my partner Clyde Pangborn."

Clyde and Preston shake hands. "I've been reading about you and this flight. A few chaps have been working behind the scenes on your behalf," Preston says.

Clyde says, "Thank you."

"Preston, how is Mother doing?" Hugh asks.

"She's fine. She wants you to know that she authorizes any help that is required for your flight."

A few minutes later, Clyde goes inside the plane. He immediately sees that something is missing.

Clyde runs back to Hugh and says, "Hugh, all the navigation charts are missing!"

Hugh says, "Maybe they got misplaced."

"You know me better than that. I would never misplace critical navigation maps. They must have been taken when we were at dinner with the mayor."

"It had to be the Black Dragons. Several were arrested last evening when they were near the plane," Preston tells the men.

Hugh asks if they can navigate by the stars.

Clyde says, "What happens when the visibility is poor or there are clouds?"

Preston says, "I didn't think they would have taken your maps."

"Hugh, you should double-check the plane. It would only take one loose bolt to spell disaster," Clyde says.

Hugh double-checks to be certain he can read the fuel gauges accurately and moves some of the fuel tanks around to be certain he can see the gauges from the manual fuel pump in the rear of the plane. He is relieved to see that everything seems to be in order.

Clyde tells him, "Always try to keep the weight of the gas equal on each side of the plane so we're not off balance."

"I'm going to be pretty busy managing the fuel."

"Let's use the five-gallon tins first. We can then discard the tins, and we don't have to worry about the tins flying through the side of the aircraft if we hit turbulence."

At the Misawa Air Base on Sunday, October 4, 1931, Japanese villagers pack down the sand with a steamroller and check the planks on the runway while Preston supervises. Preston walks up to Clyde with some paperwork in his hand.

"Here are the charts," says Preston.

"How did you get them?" asks Clyde.

"They aren't exactly the same charts. The embassy was able to provide them for the trip."

Clyde looks at the charts and says, "These should work. Thanks. Were you able to get the fuel?"

"You are fueled and ready to go," Preston answers.

A member of the aeronautical division does another check. He insists on delaying the flight until the aviation bureau can recheck the plane.

The safety checker says in Japanese, "You do not have clearance to leave. The plane must be certified."

Clyde asks Preston what he is saying.

"The plane is not certified to take off. He needs to recheck the plane."

"This is ridiculous," says Clyde.

Preston tells the safety checker from the Japanese Aviation Bureau that they are going to recheck the plane. The weight of the plane is over the airframe certification.

Clyde says, "We are thirty-four hundred pounds over the maximum allowable weight."

"We have taken out everything already. There is nothing else to do," Hugh says.

"The plane is not flight worthy and not rated for nine hundred gallons of fuel and seventy-five gallons of oil. He is not going to certify the plane," Preston says.

"Take out the radio, seat cushions, survival equipment," says Clyde.

"You can't do that. What if you need to contact us?" Preston says.

"Every pound could spell the difference between a successful takeoff or not," exclaims Clyde.

"The aeronautical bureau is concerned that you will not be able to take off," says Preston.

"Of course, it has lots of fuel. I am concerned too," says Clyde.

Preston goes to speak with the safety inspectors and then comes back.

"They want you to sign an indemnity agreement, so in case you crash, you waive any legal rights you have regarding the airworthiness of the plane," Preston says.

"Of course we will sign," says Clyde.

Black Dragon Society founder Uchida is in the crowd watching the plane being prepared for takeoff.

Uchida shouts, "They are going to be taking off soon."

Another Black Dragon says, "We have done everything possible. Somehow they were able to get the aeronautical bureau to give them permission."

"They still have to fly over Dragon's Triangle."

Later in the day, a rope is tied around the tailwheel of *Miss Veedol*.

Hugh says, "Start her up." Crowds of people are now alongside the ramp waiting for the takeoff.

The engine starts up and Hugh climbs inside. The engine is revved to full power.

As Clyde walks across the beach to board, he worries the plane will sink into the sand.

Chapter 24

The Transpacific Flight

Zero Hours

Miss Veedol, with her 425-horsepower Wasp Engine, is screaming at full power on the runway. The plane is tied by a rope to a large post.

"How fast do we have to go before we have adequate lift?" asks Hugh.

"At least ninety miles per hour," replies Clyde.

"Brakes. Check. Cut the rope."

The rope is cut as the overloaded plane lumbers down the makeshift runway. The tires of the plane bulge from the weight.

The gauges show the engine is running at full power.

"Fifty miles per hour," says Clyde.

The plane hits the packed sand but begins to get bogged down.

Clyde racks the plane from side to side to try to break the drag of the sand as they gain a little speed.

Fear is evident on Hugh's face. "Are we going to make it?"

"It is going to be close. Fifty miles per hour," says Clyde.

The pile of logs at the end of the runway is coming up fast. They still don't have enough airspeed, and most of the runway is gone.

Hugh asks, "Should we jettison fuel?"

The speedometer now says seventy miles per hour. The end of the runway is approaching.

Clyde says, "Don't jettison the fuel. It's going to be close. Ninety miles per hour."

Clyde pulls back on the yoke. The plane hits the top log and knocks it off. *Miss Veedol* seems to stall; they are airborne as the plane drops over the cliff and screams to life.

Miss Veedol drops over the edge of the cliff to just inches above the waves, and the plane stabilizes. The propeller churns the crest of the waves.

Clyde reads the airspeed out loud. It is doubtful that Hugh can hear him over the sound of the motor. "One hundred miles per hour."

They skim the surface of the water as the plane struggles to get some lift.

Clyde tells Hugh, "Start transferring fuel to the main wing tanks."

Hugh transfers the fuel from the cans to the main tank using the wobble pump.

One Hour

Hugh says, "The plane is barely flying."

"That was really close. How are you doing?" asks Clyde.

"I'm all right."

Clyde replies, "Good job, Hugh, keeping the weight balanced."

The plane is slowly gaining altitude as they head toward the Aleutian Islands.

Three Hours

They are just east of the Kuril Islands, flying at six thousand feet.

Airspeed begins to increase and the plane begins an aggressive climb.

"I'm freezing. Is there any way to keep warm?" Hugh asks, rubbing his hands on his arms.

"The engine oil circulating through the engine is beneath our seats," Clyde says.

"I can't feel any heat at all, and my fingers are going numb."

"I'm taking her up to eleven thousand feet. The engine will perform better, and there is less humidity. We shouldn't freeze up."

Hugh says, "I can't feel anything. I'm still freezing."

"Careful, Hugh. There is an insulating blanket on top of the tank so you don't get burned," Clyde cautions him.

"Thanks," Hugh says.

"We should see the Kuril Islands in the next thirty minutes. They are the last of the islands under Japanese control."

Hugh says, "It will be great to get home."

Clyde nods and checks all the instruments. "Everything is working properly. It's time for us to jettison the landing gear."

"Give me the word."

"I will put the plane into a dive so we don't risk the landing gear hitting the wing. Get ready," says Clyde.

As Clyde puts the plane into a steep dive, he motions for Hugh to pull the cables.

"Hugh, did you see the landing gear fall?"

"I don't know. I saw something fall," says Hugh.

"I can hear some wind noise. I'm going out to check."

"What do you mean you are going to check?"

"Take over the controls. Keep the plane at eleven thousand feet. Maintain speed at ninety miles per hour. I need to do a visual check," says Clyde.

Hugh takes the controls but thinks Clyde is joking. "No, really, what are you doing?"

"I will be right back."

"It's twenty degrees outside. You're going to freeze."

Hugh keeps the plane steady and Clyde climbs out the window. In the dim moonlight, eleven thousand feet above the ocean, Clyde grabs the edge of the wing strut and looks below. The struts on both sides are still there.

Clyde climbs back into the cabin of the plane and grabs a few tools.

"Both struts are still attached. The bracing rods did not fall away."

Hugh is surprised since he saw the mechanism tested. "You tested them many times."

Clyde thinks for a moment about what could have gone wrong. "They must have gotten damaged on takeoff."

Hugh is oblivious to the risk of landing with the struts in place. "They should be all right for landing."

Clyde doesn't want to worry Hugh. However, he knows from experience that they can't land with the struts attached. "If we land with the struts the way they are, they will rip through the cabin and tear us and plane apart. I have to go back out there."

"You can't go back out there. It's too dangerous."

"I will work them free. Just hold the plane steady and I'll finish the job."

He hangs onto the wing strut with one hand. With the other hand, he unbolts the strut, then loosens it, and it falls away from the plane.

Clyde shivers. Because it is freezing, he almost loses his grip on the wing, but he catches himself. He falls back inside the plane, trembling.

"Are you all right, Clyde?"

"I have to go back out."

"Why don't you wait?"

"I'm going to finish the job."

The wind rushes by Clyde at ninety miles per hour.

He climbs outside from the port cockpit window and steps onto the wing strut. Below him is nothing but darkness.

He hangs on with one hand, and with the other, he unbolts the second strut from the airframe, and it drops off the plane.

He makes it back to the window and climbs back inside the plane, frozen and shaking.

Hugh helps him through the window, and the plane veers to the left. Hugh moves immediately into his seat and gets the plane under control.

Clyde has some overexposure and is shivering, so Hugh continues to fly the plane.

Everything inside the plane is freezing. Outside everything is grey and dark. The window is cracked open to provide some ventilation.

Four Hours

Hugh says, "You did it."

"Take her up to fourteen thousand feet. We should pick up a tail wind."

"Are you all right?" Hugh asks him.

"I am closing my eyes. Wake me up in an hour."

Five Hours

It is pitch-dark except for the crescent moon lingering in the sky. Clyde is still sleeping.

Eight Hours

Clyde wakes up and says, "How long have I been asleep?"

"A couple hours."

"I'll take over now. We need to pump more fuel into the main fuel tank. Let's jettison the empty fuel cans now," Clyde says.

"Ready when you are."

"All right. Open the starboard window. I'll pitch the plane to the side while you throw the cans out. Remember, we've got to be careful about throwing them out so they don't hit the rear wing. Here we go."

Clyde pitches the plane and Hugh starts to throw out the cans.

Ten Hours

The moon is in the star-lit sky surrounded by clouds as the plane starts to shake violently. Clyde has gone to sleep again, and Hugh shouts to him, "Clyde, wake up!"

Clyde opens his eyes, fully awake in an instant. "Why is the plane shaking?"

Hugh says, "I don't know."

"I need to take the controls. The wings are icing up."

"What are we going to do?" Hugh asks.

"We're going to seventeen thousand feet. We should stay ice free and the air should be smooth."

Hugh checks the drinking water. "The water in the canteens has frozen."

Clyde is focused on the job at hand and almost oblivious to the extreme cold. "Position check. There is a volcano directly below us. Do you see it?"

Hugh looks down and sees the volcano. "Check."

"Remember to keep those main wing tanks topped off," Clyde reminds him.

Hugh operates the wobble pump in slow motion with his nearly frozen hands.

"Maybe it's the altitude, but I can't keep my eyes open," Hugh says.

The engine begins to sputter, and the single-engine plane's propellers slow down and almost stop. The plane begins to lose altitude.

Hugh starts to pump faster to transfer the fuel.

"That was close, Hugh. We don't have an electric starter if the engine stops!"

Fifteen Hours
Over the Aleutians

In the middle of the night, a ham radio operator inside his cabin hears the sound of a sputtering engine. "At 3:15 a.m., I just heard the sounds of an airplane overhead, flying over the Aleutian Islands."

The other radio operator says, "Thank you. Roger and out."

Sixteen Hours
Pangborn's Mother's House
Wenatchee, WA

The phone rings, and Clyde's mother, Opal, goes to answer the wall-mounted phone.

"Hello," she says.

The radio operator says, "We just received word from a ham radio operator that an airplane was heard over the Aleutian Islands. We believe it was from Clyde's airplane."

"It must be him. There aren't many airplanes flying over the Aleutians," she says, happy to hear he is safe.

"I just wanted to let you know. I'll call you if I hear anything else."

"Thank you. I really appreciate it. By the way, there are about thirty people at the airport here in Washington waiting for him in case he decides to land here. Does anyone know where Clyde is going to land?" his mother asks.

"No, they just think that he might land here since there is a thick fog over the coast."

"Thank you again for calling," Opal says as she hangs up the phone.

Diane waits impatiently to hear what Opal has to say. "Is Clyde all right?"

"He is somewhere over the Aleutian Islands. A ham radio operator just heard a plane flying over the islands."

"How do you stay so calm?"

"I am worried, just like you."

"I can't really take it," Diane says, wringing her hands.

"It is hard for me too, thinking of him up there. It has always been like that with Clyde. I just pray that he will be all right."

"I am so happy to be here with you. I just don't know if I could have a life like this, always worrying if he will come home safely."

"It is hard always be worrying. And the more you love them, the more you worry."

Diane nods. "I worry about him a lot."

Twenty Hours

It is late afternoon as they fly near Attu Island in the Aleutian Island chain, and they see land for the first time.

Hugh is sleeping as they eventually fly over the Gulf of Alaska.

"Wake up, Hugh. The Aleutian Islands."

"How much longer do we have?"

"We are about halfway there. That is Attu Island down below. We will cross the International Date Line in several hours."

"I need a cigarette and some coffee."

Clyde laughs. "Just make sure we have fuel in the tanks, Hugh."

Twenty-Eight Hours

The weather is clear, and Saint Elias Mountain is imposing, at eighteen thousand feet high, as it comes out of the low-lying clouds.

Hugh barely wakes up to look around sleepily and say, "Where are we?"

Clyde tells him, "We are over Kayak Island. That is Saint Elias Mountain there in the distance. It's the second-highest mountain in America next to Mount McKinley," and Hugh falls back to sleep.

The engine starts to stutter again and then completely shuts down. "Hugh!"

No answer.

Clyde shouts, "Hugh! Wake up."

Clyde puts the plane into a dive to get some fuel into the engine. Nothing.

Clyde reaches over and hits Hugh in the head with his fist.

Over the ocean, the engine coughs. Clyde stretches to view the glass fuel tube.

Clyde shouts, "Hugh, we're out of gas!"

Finally coming out of his sleep state, Hugh says, "What the hell?"

"You idiot, the engine just died!"

"What are we going to do?"

"Better start pumping right now."

Hugh springs into action and starts rapidly pumping gasoline.

Clyde tilts the aircraft into a steep dive again. The sun is coming up over the horizon.

"What are you doing?" Hugh yells.

"Just keep pumping, Hugh."

Hugh starts to cry. "What are you doing?" Hugh sobs. "We're going to die. The legend is true."

The airspeed indicator registers 120 miles per hour, then 140, and then 160. The plane is shaking and becomes unstable.

Hugh shouts, "Clyde, what are you doing? The plane isn't rated for this."

"What difference does it make? The engine starts or that's it." Clyde knew all along that the choices were limited.

"Hang on. The air is getting thicker. Five thousand feet."

Hugh watches the speed indicator hit 180, then 190, and climb to 200. "We're going to die."

"Hope that the wings don't fall off. Four thousand feet. Three thousand feet."

"I'm sorry, Clyde."

The plane is shaking violently and the interior begins to fall apart. Hugh continues to pump, and Clyde pitches the plane to get the remaining fuel into the fuel lines. The icy-cold grey water is quickly approaching.

"Two thousand feet," Clyde warns.

The propeller starts to spin. There is a loud explosion and smoke comes from the engine as it backfires.

There is another loud explosion and the engine comes to life. To Hugh and Clyde, it sounds as if the plane and engine have just fallen apart. Hugh's eyes are closed.

Clyde pulls up to level the plane but not so steeply as to sheer the wings off.

"One thousand feet," Clyde says as he begins to pull the plane out of the dive.

Tears stream down Hugh's face, and he screams out of fear. "Did we make it?"

"Keep pumping."

"Over there. That mountain peak looks like the Dragon's Triangle," Hugh says, pointing to a mountain peak in the shape of a triangle looming in the distance.

The plane starts the ascent after it barely misses the ground and low-lying trees.

Hugh is still sobbing and wipes the tears from his eyes.

"We did it," he says.

Clyde is stoic. "Yeah, we did it. Keep on pumping."

"We beat the dragon."

"If there is a dragon, we still have a long way to go," Clyde says.

From the Kayak Island lighthouse, a radio operator radios to another operator that he heard an airplane.

Thirty Hours

Clyde hasn't spoken a word for many hours when Hugh finally breaks the silence.

"Where are we now?"

"We are off the coast of Canada. This is probably the Queen Charlotte Islands."

"How long have we been flying?"

"We've been airborne for about thirty hours. I need to sleep for a couple hours."

"All right. I feel awake now."

"Do we have enough fuel in the main tank for a few hours?" Clyde asks.

"Yes."

"Hold the current altitude and speed. Don't go off course. If you stay at this heading, wake me when you see lights below. That should be Vancouver."

"All right."

Clyde immediately falls fast asleep.

Thirty-Two Hours

"Wake up, Clyde," Hugh calls.

"Are we over Vancouver? I can't see with all the clouds."

"We're over Vancouver?" Hugh asks, confused.

Clyde looks out the window, and he sees a snow-covered mountain just in front of them. Clyde reaches over and grabs the controls, and the plane goes into a steep turn.

Mt. Rainier is right in front of them. It is over 14,400 feet high and one of the most dangerous volcanoes in the world. The mountain is covered with fog. If a pilot is not watching out and expecting the mountain, it would be easy to run into it.

The plane completes a sharp turn and barely misses crashing straight into the side of the mountain.

Hugh breathes a sigh of relief. "That was close. Where are we?"

Clyde laughs, and he asks Hugh, "How is it possible to miss both Vancouver and Seattle and almost crash into a mountain?"

"I don't know."

"I think it's Mount Rainier. We are only about a couple hundred miles off course," Clyde says and takes a looks at his map. "How's our gas?"

"We have about a hundred gallons of fuel left."

"Pump the remaining fuel to the center tank. We're flying to Boise, Idaho."

Thirty-Five Hours
Over Boise, Idaho

It's nighttime when Clyde asks, "How are we doing on fuel now?"

"We still have at least fifty gallons."

"All right."

"We should be over Boise now, right?" Hugh asks.

"Look down below. We are over Boise. Do you see anything?"

"I just see clouds."

"Is it just clouds, or do you see fog?" Clyde asks.

"It looks like there is heavy fog. I can't see anything."

"We can't land here. I can't see a thing and we could run into a tree. We have to go back to Washington. It's clear there."

Miss Veedol bounces around as the weather continues to get worse.

Forty Hours
Over Wenatchee, Washington

It's 6:30 in the morning, and it has been four hours since someone reported hearing a plane over Seattle.

Diane says, "They should be here by now."

"Don't worry. He's all right," Opal says.

"But it has been over four hours, and no one has heard from them." Diane sighs heavily.

Opal pats her on the knee. "I know my son. He's looking for a safe area to land the plane."

Forty-One Hours
October 5, 1931 at 7:14 a.m.

The plane swoops over the hills and circles the airfield. Clyde tells Hugh to dump the remaining fuel.

Hugh says, "What if we need to make another pass?"

"Dump the fuel. I want to make sure we don't burn up. I'm shutting off the ignition," Clyde explains.

The fuel is emptied, and the plane becomes a glider as the propeller continues to spin. The propeller stops right in position so it won't hit the runway when they land.

Everything is going well, but at the last moment, a gust of wind hits the plane and the propeller make a quarter turn.

Clyde calls out, "Get ready for a crash landing, Hugh. Fasten your seat-belt."

"We're going to flip!" Hugh says.

"We're going to be fine. I am going to keep the nose up as long as possible," Clyde tells him.

The Bellanca is close to stalling. The plane comes in nose up. The tail drags and the airframe starts to shake violently. Sparks are flying out.

The nose digs in, and the plane turns in a cloud of dust and skids along for another one hundred feet before it stops. It lingers for a moment and then falls onto its left wing tip.

A small crowd of thirty people run toward the plane.

Clyde tells Hugh, "We did it. Congratulations. We flew forty-five hundred miles in forty-one hours thirteen minutes."

Hugh coldly replies, "Congratulations. You know you can't talk about the trip, right?."

"What are you talking about?"

"There is a gag order. It's all in those papers you signed. You can't talk about the trip for one year."

"What are you saying? I can't speak about the journey we took?"

"Sorry, country boy. You speak about the trip and you end up losing everything."

"Hugh, you are one of the worst people I have ever met in my life."

Hugh laughs. "We get any award money too."

As Clyde and Hugh jump out of the plane, photographers begin to take photos and Opal and Diane immediately run up and hug Clyde. Hugh poses for pictures by the plane.

Clyde is happy to see his mother and Diane. He asks, "What are you doing here? How did you know where I would land?"

"I just thought you might land here. Intuition, I guess."

"I have been staying with your mother," Diane says.

Clyde smiles. "See. I promised I would come back."

"I didn't know how difficult it would be waiting for you."

Chapter 25

A representative of the Japanese newspaper *Asahi Shimbun* steps forward. "I am here to present Alice Boardman with a check in the amount of fifty thousand dollars."

Impressed, Hugh says, "That would be my mother."

"She is listed as a sponsor of the trip. It is with great honor that I present the check to you as Alice Boardman's son."

Hugh takes the check and says, "Thank you very much. It was a difficult trip. My mother is honored to receive the check from you. We planned the trip for a long time and are pleased that we reached our goal."

The photographers take pictures of Hugh and the newspaper's representative.

Clyde asks the representative, "How did you know we would land here?"

"We guessed your most likely landing point. How do you feel?"

"It was a long flight. We are both tired. We accomplished what we set out to do," Clyde says.

Hugh whispers to Clyde, "Remember, any interviews with news media and my family will see you in court." Hugh smiles to the reporters and photographers.

A reporter from the *Seattle News* named Carl steps forward to ask Clyde a few questions. "We would like to ask you a few questions about your achievement."

Clyde smirks at Hugh. "I am rather tired after being in the air for over forty-one hours. Why don't you speak with Hugh?"

Hugh says, "Right now, I am happy to be home."

Chapter 26

Opal's Home
Wenatchee, WA

Several months later, a reporter from the *New York Times Union* comes to speak with Clyde.

Opal answers the door and says, "Good morning. What can I do for you?"

"Good morning. I'm from the *New York Times*, and I'd like to speak with Clyde."

"Please take a seat out on the veranda."

"Thank you. I'd love to sit on the veranda and enjoy the beautiful day," he says as he takes a seat on a wicker rocking chair.

"I'll be right back," Opal says and goes back into the house.

Clyde comes out and stands in the doorway, not saying anything. He's not one for small talk.

The reporter stands, holding his hand out to shake Clyde's, and introduces himself.

A moment later, Opal comes out with some mint julep tea.

The reporter and Opal enjoy a lively conversation, and Clyde warms up to him in his quiet way.

Clyde finally says something. "You didn't have to come all the way out here to speak with me."

"Your partner has been giving many interviews regarding your flight. In all the interviews, he has said that you were assisting him in the journey. We would love to hear from you regarding the trip."

Clyde realizes this is the time to tell his story. However, he knows, by this time, the public is no longer interested in the story since the flight is old news.

Clyde looks at the report straight in the eye. "You have come a long way to speak with me. What would you like to know?"

"Who did most of the flying during the trip?" asks the reporter.

"Out of the two hundred hours flying since we left New York, I flew about one hundred ninety hours. The flight logs will confirm this."

"Herndon said in an interview that he navigated while you were flying the aircraft."

"Hugh was able to keep us on course occasionally," Clyde says, chuckling.

"How much money did you personally receive from the trip?"

"At this point, I haven't received anything. The *Asahi Shimbun* prize money was paid to Alice Boardman as the sponsor of the trip."

"Do you hold any ill will toward your flying partner?" asks the reporter.

"Of course not. I love what I do. I am a pilot, and I do it to the best of my ability."

"Why have you not given any interviews before this one?"

"They had a gag order in place, so I wasn't allowed to speak with anyone for a short while," says Clyde.

The reporter continues to ask Clyde questions about being a prisoner in Japan for seven weeks, how the Japanese treated them, the journey, the people who helped them, the plane and their modifications, and about running out of fuel. Clyde felt a bit better after getting it all off his chest.

By the time Clyde's version of the story was published, it was old news. Amelia Earhart's cross-country records was big news in 1931 and 1932, dominating the headlines, and very few people ever heard of the first nonstop transpacific flight.

S P E C I F I C A T I O N

LONG-DISTANCE BELLANCA PLANE
for
MR. EMIL ROTH, JR.

Airplane:
Fuselage - special long-distance with Pacemaker landing gear.
Cabin interior same as previous long-distance ships.
Standard float gear attachment fittings and hoist lugs on fuselage.

Wings:
J-type.

Gasoline Tanks:
Fuselage tanks to be equipped with eight-inch diameter quick opening and closing dump valves operated by passenger. Total gasoline capacity to be 700 gallons, including 100 gallons in cans.

Fuel System:
Fuel engine pump and hand pump. All gasoline line connections taped.

Oil Tank:
One 15-gallon (minimum) tank under pilot seat of such height that pilot and passenger can sit on it; two 5-gallon cans.

Controls:
Standard Pacemaker.

Cabin Arrangement:
No cabin doors. Small floor behind tank. Zipper opening in top and on each side, rear of tank.

Instruments:
Blank instrument board to be sent to Pioneer Instrument Company who will install the instruments at the Bellanca Company's expense, but in locations to be agreed upon between the purchaser and the Pioneer Instrument Company. Instruments furnished: Pioneer Earth Inductor Compass, small-type Aperiodic Compass (on bracket in suitable position), Rieker pitch indicator, altimeter, air speed indicator, tachometer, rate-of-climb indicator, oil thermometer, oil pressure gauge, two bank and turn indicators, gasoline level gauges on gravity tanks only.

Propellor:
Hamilton-Standard Metal.

Lights:
Navigation lights with smallest power bulbs, and instrument board lights, complete with three dry cells, to be supplied by purchaser.

Finish:
Pigmented dope, Orange (make to be specified by purchaser).

Engine:
Wright J-6 Super-Inspected, with rocker arm lubrication led to cockpit for each cylinder. Ring Cowl.

This specification has been agreed to and is to be incorporated as part of the order as signed January 22, 1931.

BELLANCA AIRCRAFT CORPORATION

By: _____
Title: _____

Agreed to:

_____, January   , 1931.

Epilogue

During World War II, Clyde joined the Royal Air Force and fought for England in the battle for Britain. He flew one hundred seventy airplanes across the Atlantic during the war without a single incident and continued to work for the airlines as a test pilot after the war.

After WWII, Clyde returned to Misawa, Japan. As a gift to the people of Misawa City, Clyde brought five cuttings from Washington State's famed Red Delicious apples from the mayor of Wenatchee. They were grafted onto trees in Misawa City and distributed to apple growers throughout Japan. Clyde never saw Yumiko or Yosh again. He went back to Japan to find them after the war, but he was never able to find them.

During the war, Yosh and Yumiko went to Nagasaki, Japan, to help in the war effort during the 1940s. They were in Nagasaki on August 9, 1945, when the second atom bomb exploded over Nagasaki. They were never seen again.

Clyde received $2,500 for his transatlantic flight and other aviation awards, including the Harmon Trophy with aviation greats as Charles Lindbergh and Jimmy Doolittle. Japan congratulated Pangborn and awarded him the Imperial Aeronautical Medal of Merit.

In 1934, Clyde flew in the MacRobertson Race from London to Australia with a time of ninety-two hours and fifty-five minutes, flying a Boeing 234D "Warner Bros" Comet.

Clyde never lost a plane. On March 29, 1958, Clyde died at the age of sixty-three. He is buried in Arlington National Cemetery with full military honors.

Hugh Herndon became a captain in the Royal Canadian Air Force. After WWII, he became chief pilot in the African–Middle East section for Transcontinental and Western airline, which later became TWA. He got divorced from Mary Ellen Farley. They had two daughters together. He later married Ruth Dainty. He died of a stroke in 1952 in Cairo, Egypt, at the age of fifty-three. Hugh and Clyde never spoke again.

Diane Bronson and Clyde did not end up staying together. She married a surgeon from the hospital where she worked. They moved to Methow Valley, fifty miles outside of Wenatchee.

Miss Veedol was sold and used for transatlantic flights. In 1932, *Miss Veedol* left Floyd Bennett Field in New York for Rome and was never see again.

Giuseppe Bellanca was on the cover of *Time* magazine on July 4, 1927. He formed the Bellanca Aircraft Corporation in a partnership with the DuPont family. During WWII, he designed cargo planes, and in 1954, formed Bellanca Development Company. He died of cancer in New York on December 26, 1960, at the age of seventy-four.

About the Author

David Rosten studied Scandinavian history at UCLA and at the University of Copenhagen. Mr. Rosten has degrees in political science and international and comparative law. He is on the community board of directors for the Center of Citizenpeacebuilding, Department of Social Sciences at the University of California and on the national board of directors for the Olive Tree Initiative at UC Irvine. He is former cochair of the Dean's Council at UC Irvine. He currently lives in Newport Beach with his two dogs and his children.

Edwards Brothers Malloy
Thorofare, NJ USA
December 7, 2015